The dark at the top of the stairs . . .

Matches—she had to light the lamp. There were none. She opened the door. Nervous at the thought of darkness above the first turn, she started up. She could no longer see her hands. Primal fear of darkness made her heart pound loudly, until she heard the voices from above. *It must be the attic.*

The voices came more strongly, the first an indistinguishable mumble, followed by the clear words of a girl—Corliss. "I don't care! I like her, no matter what Skelly says. You can't hurt her—I won't let you!"

Marla froze. *She doesn't mean you . . . they're not talking about you.*

Mumble. Skelly? No, Corliss's words had made it clear that she was talking to someone else. What was going on up there? Who was Corliss talking to? Silence now; then the mumbler spoke again. Although the words couldn't be deciphered, she was sure the speaker was a boy.

Then Corliss: "No, Andrew!" *Thank you for identifying him, Corliss.* "You can't! If you do, I'll never come back!"

The mumble again, more forceful, derisive.

Corliss, triumphant. "No, he won't! I won't let Skelly come either—you know he does whatever I say. We'll both stay away, and you'll be all alone again."

A dull sound, moving away. The participants had left. Who was Andrew? She hadn't heard there was another child at Beechhaven. The son of one of the servants? Not likely.

And then, with horror, she remembered Corliss saying, "We'll both stay away and you'll be all alone again."

There was a little boy in the attic. Was he a prisoner there? In the dark? Did anyone besides the children know?

What was going on in that strange house?

The Attic Child

Grace Corren

PINNACLE BOOKS • LOS ANGELES

This is a work of fiction. All the characters and events portrayed in this book are fictional, and any resemblance to real people or incidents is purely coincidental.

THE ATTIC CHILD

An original Pinnacle Books edition, published for the first time anywhere.

First printing, September 1979

ISBN: 0-523-40322-4

Cover illustration by Jack Thurston

Printed in the United States of America

PINNACLE BOOKS, INC.
2029 Century Park East
Los Angeles, California 90067

THE ATTIC CHILD

One

9:00 A.M. The potbellied stove in the waiting room radiated heat, although the only fire was in the sun pouring through the grimy windows. Somewhere nearby, an insect droned, competing with the measured tick of the fly-specked clock over the ticket window. Somewhere outside, conversation stuttered into life, then broke off again. It was too hot for talking. Almost too hot for breathing.

9:00 A.M., Wednesday, July 1, 1942.

Marla Doren yawned, jaw cracking, and shifted on the hard bench, her blouse sticking to her back. She searched her purse and found a handkerchief, which she used to wipe her face, and succeeded in smearing the soot mark trailing from the corner of one hazel eye across her high-arched cheekbone. Feeling sticky-dirty, she stuffed the bit of cloth back into her pale green alligator handbag and moved it from her lap to the bench. The corner of Garman Gibson's letter peeked through the brass clasps.

9:00 A.M., eastern war time. Stifling another yawn, Marla checked her watch against the station clock, then leaned back and closed her eyes. What time was it in real life? Confused, she thought for a moment, then decided it was only seven. And already so hot. She balled her fist and pressed her knuckles against her teeth, blinking against sleep grit in the corners of her eyes.

Another yawn split her face, and she fought the urge to stretch out on the slats of the curved bench and give in to her intense need for sleep. On this, the sixth day of the first real heat wave of summer, the humidity was near saturation. And there was an out-of-order sign on the ladies'-room door. She couldn't even wash her face, unless she walked up to the village. The thought was tempting, but Marla was too tired. Another glance touched the clock, and she wondered how long it would be before her already-late train arrived.

She sighed and let her head roll slowly, easing the ache in her neck. Unable to sleep last night, Marla had checked the thermometer at three this morning; it had been eighty-six degrees then. Earlier, heat lightning had teased in the west, but the real storm had stayed far away over Lake Ontario. Now the early morning sun stood copper in the flawless blue sky.

Marla, a pretty girl of twenty-two, was alone in the Remsen train station; the half-dozen other passengers were waiting out on the platform, in the futile hope of a cooling breeze. At least they were shielded from the climbing sun. She wondered if she should join them, but the effort seemed too great.

Her eyes closed again, and her face was nearly hidden by the broad-brimmed, starched linen hat that matched her purse. Long blond hair was carefully gathered at the neck. Only the soot

streak marred her oval features, until someone
came close enough to see through the shadow of
the hat to the haggard lines around her eyes.
Despite her exhaustion, she drew approving
glances from two men who slowed their pace to
allow a quick look through the door.

A whistle sounded from the troop train that
had been tying up the yard for the last twenty
minutes. It was a tired sound, as though even the
machinery were reluctant to operate in the heat.
The train moved, clattering and banging as car
couplings slammed together, then crashed apart.
Marla stood, straightened her skirt, and moved to
the station door, where she watched the young
soldiers leaning out the windows of the train,
waving and laughing at the civilians on the platform. Two bristle-haired teenage boys spotted
Marla, shouted, and waved at her.

The train rounded the curve out of the yard
limits, heading toward Pine Camp, eighty miles
to the north. The mournful whistle challenged a
crossroads. Twenty-four miles, three station stops,
and the soldiers would pass through Lyons Falls
. . . Marla's home village. She wished she were on
it, riding back. . . .

Another whistle sounded from the south and a
yard worker in bib overalls and a blue and white
striped cap crossed the tracks to throw the
switch. Marla turned and saw the locomotive of
the passenger train belching black smoke as it
pulled into the place vacated by the army train.
The odor of soft coal was suddenly sharper.

As Marla turned back from the door to gather
up her purse and her pale green linen jacket,
which matched her skirt, the telegraph key began

a furious clicking. Her bags were already on the platform. She moved outside as the stationmaster brushed past, hurrying to answer the key. He muttered something, which Marla was just as glad she couldn't understand, and the stink of chewing tobacco moved with him like a cloud. She held her breath, fighting her stomach.

The locomotive stopped, steam spilling from its undercarriage, as a roly-poly conductor dropped his stool from the second of the six passenger cars. He stepped down and turned to help a woman off the train. Three cars back, the brakeman too dropped his stool, but the woman was the only passenger getting off. The conductor looked both ways, then bellowed:

"Old Forge, Racquet Lake, Eagle Bay, points *north*!"

Four passengers climbed into the train while Marla picked up her suitcases. She looked down the length of the train and felt her heart sink; every window seat was occupied, although only a few people were curious enough to stare out at the small village station, and she could see more passengers standing in the aisles.

"Mornin', miss. Step careful, please."

"Good-morning," Marla replied, as the conductor took her bags and swung them up into the vestibule. "Is there any hope of a seat?"

"Not right now. How far you goin'?"

"Beechhaven."

He shook his head. "Not before Old Forge. We're three cars short when we could use some extra. People been standin' since Utica."

Uttering a small sigh, Marla stepped onto the

stool and climbed the three steps into the train. "It's Wednesday," she said, "why so crowded?"

"First of July. Most of this lot's up from New York City, startin' summer vacation."

The stationmaster came out and hurried by with green flimsies on a clasp pole—orders for the engineer. The conductor bent to scan the undercarriage, a halfhearted effort that ignored the cars ahead and behind, then signaled to the brakeman, to the conductor, and finally to the engineer in the locomotive, who responded by leaning on the whistle.

"Awwwww *'board!*"

The conductor picked up his stool and swung up onto the steps, the quick movement belying his tubby appearance. The whistle sounded again while the train chattered for a few seconds, then began to move, the jerk nearly throwing Marla off-balance.

"Sorry 'bout that, miss." The conductor caught her arm, steadying her. "Troop train's got us almost an hour behind schedule."

"Will we make up any time?"

"Once through the junction and on the Adirondack Division we'll pick up some. You can't stay out here, though. It ain't safe."

Sighing, Marla moved out of the way to let him drop the iron shield over the steps. The doors stood open between the cars; she looked ahead and saw the aisle crowded, with several men and older boys standing or perched on the arms of the seats.

The car immediately behind was just as congested, but prospects for the next car back seemed better. Marla gathered her bags, squeezing purse

5

between arm and side, and struggled into the car, reaping dirty looks whenever her suitcases hit seats or bodies. Blushing with embarrassment, she fought her way through the car. The conductor followed her as far as the door, where he turned and started forward again.

"Tickets, please! Tickets!"

Except for one boy perched on the arm of his mother's seat, the aisle of this car was clear, but there were no empty seats. Marla paused in her flight for control of her burden of luggage, biting her lip as she scanned the next car back. It seemed no better, but she picked up the struggle again, muttering shamefaced apologies each time the lurching train made her bump into someone.

Halfway back, a man slumped with one knee cocked into the aisle, his hat pulled down over his face. Marla glowered, as jealous of his ability to sleep as of his seat. The train was picking up speed as it moved toward the switch from the St. Lawrence Division of the New York Central Railroad. Marla pushed through the aisle more easily as she found the rhythm of the train, and was turning sideways to sidle past the sleeping man when the car lurched as it hit the switch.

"Oh!" She staggered and hit the seat behind her, then the car lurched again and threw her in the other direction. Her small suitcase slammed into the sleeper's gut.

"Hey! Watch it, you—"

He doubled over, holding his stomach, and whatever he had been about to say was cut off as he saw his attacker's legs. He struggled erect and pushed the suitcase back at Marla. Unprepared, she nearly fell into the lap of the woman in the next seat back.

Marla muttered another embarrassed apology and struggled to her feet again, while the man pushed his hat back from his face and sat up.

"What's the matter with you, sister?"

"I said I was sorry!"

Her anger was flaring as she bent to retrieve her purse and jacket, juggling the suitcases—but the train chose that moment to lurch again. She fell to her knees and everything scattered, the contents of her purse skidding out into the aisle. Change rolled in every direction, and tears stabbed at her eyes.

"No, *No*!"

"Hey, take it—*Marla*?"

Astonished at hearing someone call her name, she looked up, giving up the struggle to stop the rolling coins. She blinked rapidly against her tears and for the first time saw his face. It was her turn to stare.

"*Tim*?"

Seconds passed while their eyes met, and then a broad smile spread across his face. He scrambled out of his seat and bent to help Marla collect the contents of her purse; half a minute later, almost bumping heads, he stood up and pressed the last errant nickle into her hand.

"Well." He cocked his head. "Just get on at Remsen?"

"Yes ... yes, I did."

Marla snapped her purse shut and struggled up from her knees as Tim scanned the car. Seeing no empty seats, he picked up her large suitcase and forced it into the rack over his seat, turning it sideways so that it would fit. There was no room for the smaller case.

"Here, sit down. Watch your feet—I'll have to squeeze this in here."

Marla sank down gratefully, spreading her feet to let Tim wedge the bag between them. Her head fell back and she sighed, conscious of one bruised knee. Her eyes shut of their own volition, and she left them that way for a moment. Then she looked up as her seat companion shifted.

"Oh!" She jerked her arm away from the stab of wool fiber and stared in astonishment. The man beside her was a bearded lumberjack, sleeping, clad in wool pants and wool shirt. The heat obviously didn't bother him.

Tim grinned. "Unless you want a cheap drunk, don't inhale too deeply."

Her nose wrinkled, but she was too tired to consider. Marla edged away carefully, and the lumberjack shifted position again, shrugging into the corner.

"So tell me," said Tim, "what are you doing here?"

"I could ask the same of you. We heard you were in the army."

Tim smiled again, glancing down at his rumpled seersucker suit, and clinging precariously to the back of Marla's seat as the train swayed again, rounding a curve.

"I offered, but Uncle Sam said thanks but no thanks."

"What happened?" As soon as the words were out Marla regretted them, but Tim seemed not to share her embarrassment.

"Something silly—a hole in my eardrum, or a

8

heart murmur. Just enough to keep me safely civilian. I was just as happy. Duty called and Mrs. Layard's son Timothy answered, but I never was keen on going where the bang-bangs are for real."

Marla thought of the troop train heading north, the youngsters riding in it. Tim's words seemed callous. Then she glanced at his eyes and saw the furrowed brow that meant he was trying to hide his feelings. She remembered the Tim Layard she used to know. It had always been his way to make jokes of the things that mattered most. He had volunteered; that was to his credit. At least he hadn't tried to dodge the draft like some she knew.

As Marla studied Tim, four years fell away. . . .

The last time she had been with Tim was at the Labor Day dance—the end of summer, 1938. Four years ago, after three years of constantly being together.

She marveled at the thought. In that long-ago time, it had seemed that they had always been together and always would be together. Marla Doren and Tim Layard, the perfect match, a lifetime pair. *Everyone* knew it. . . .

Everyone, apparently, except Tim.

The memories came back in a rush, released from the dark closet where she had locked them away after the tears and regrets were finally done. She had known it was ending even before Tim found the courage to tell her. All that summer he had been distant, although they dated as frequently as ever. Tim would soon be returning to his junior year at college, and Marla had just graduated from high school.

She blinked and picked a particle of train soot from her eyelashes. Marla had worn Tim's fraternity pin since the weekend he had come home pledged, and his high-school class ring before then. She still had both of them, someplace; Tim had never asked for them back. Everyone knew it was only a matter of time before a diamond took their place on her left hand. Everyone . . .

Marla let her head fall back and closed her eyes as the memories of happier days flooded back. When had the change in him begun, become apparent? She recalled now the days of that last summer and the way it had been during the summers before 1938. They had vowed undying love for each other. . . .

When did he first say he loved her? In 1936, yes—after a hot-dog roast along the dunes. Tim was about to leave for his first year at the university, his future assured. He drew Marla away from the others and held her close. That night the phrase came haltingly, for Tim was embarrassed, although with time it became easier. He said it often after that night, almost every time they met.

That was the first time . . . when was the last?

Spring, 1938: a miserable, cold April, new rains mixing with the remnants of old snow to turn the whole world gray and sodden. Tim was home for the funeral of his parents; now he was alone in the world, except for Marla.

She stood by his side as the minister droned through the last service, but even then she was aware of the change in him. The death of his only

10

relatives in a terrible car crash was not the cata-
lyst. No; she knew he had met someone else,
someone at the university. For a time Marla
fooled herself into thinking that nothing had
changed, that he still loved her; but she had
never been good at self-deception.

She yawned again and opened her eyes, massaging the cords of her throat to ease the sharp
stab of pain as her jaw cracked.

"Is something wrong, Marla?"

"What?" His question startled her. "Oh, no."

"Jaw still pop out on you?"

She smiled. "Yes. Silly, isn't it? Why couldn't I
have something useful, like a double-jointed
thumb?"

Tim eased himself onto the arm of the seat,
Marla edging over until her elbow brushed
against the sleeping lumberjack. She shrugged
away, her left shoulder resting against Tim's
comfortable bulk, and closed her eyes again. She
thought back to 1938. She remembered clearly:
Labor Day, the end of a long weekend of celebra-
tion. A frantic weekend, as Tim rushed her about
the countryside, trying to fill three days with
weeks of fun.

But she had known that they had come to the
end of their comfortable relationship. . . .

After the dance Tim said he had something to
say, but he was silent for a long time before the
words came out. Marla resisted her impulse to
put her hand over his lips to stop the damnable
confession.

"I'm not coming back to Lyons Falls again."

Numbed, she listened. It was almost two in the
morning and the streets were deserted. They

were parked outside her house, sitting in the front seat of his father's new Oldsmobile, while Tim tried to find the words to explain his decision. His Oldsmobile now, she thought, distracted.

"There's nothing here for me, Marla."

(Not even me?) But the lament remained unvoiced.

"Where will you go? What will you do?"

"For now, back to school. After that I don't know. I do know I don't want to take over Dad's insurance business—I'm selling the agency. Selling the house, too."

"Isn't that rather . . . drastic?"

(And sudden?) But, like the lament, it remained unsaid.

"I don't think so. What's here for me? I'm not the type to go into the paper mill; I don't want to be a papermaker the rest of my life. And I certainly wasn't cut out to be a farmer. What else does Lyons Falls have?"

(Me! Me! Me . . .)

Marla heard him out without argument. When the words stopped, he had said nothing of her, and it wasn't necessary to press the point. If there had still been a place in his future for Marla Doren, he would have said so.

Marla accepted his last kiss, although neither of them said good-bye, the life drained from her responses. Then she broke away, tears blinding her as she stumbled out of the car and ran to the house. She knew he was relieved that she did not look back.

Four years had passed, yet she could recall every word of their last conversation as though it had taken place yesterday. For a time Tim had continued to write inconsequential notes, but Marla never answered. By Christmas the letters stopped, saving them both further embarrassment.

But now Tim was beside her, touching her. . . .

Marla's throat worked and she felt the sting of tears. She looked up at him, but his eyes were closed.

She studied his face: he had changed. Four years is a long time for the young. His features seemed sharper and more angular with the maturity that had not yet come at twenty. He was combing his dark brown hair in a different style, and he needed a shave.

"Mmm!"

He opened his eyes to shake his head once and made a face; then smiled at her. "Smell the coal. Makes me sorry I grabbed breakfast."

"Are you all right?"

"I'll survive. It won't be more than a couple of hours."

Marla yawned herself, and the momentary twinge of guilt at taking his seat vanished. How could he be more tired than she? She felt the weight of his presence as Tim let his arm rest across the top of the seat and settled herself lower, looking up at him again.

But some things had not changed. She remembered that scar on his chin, barely visible unless you knew just where to look; then it jumped out at you, a sharp white line. It was the souvenir of a bicycle accident when Tim was thirteen.

And his eyes, lined with fatigue, were still deep brown and deeply hypnotic—the eyes of a born salesman like his father. Tim was a natural leader, could always talk others into doing whatever he wanted.

In 1938 he had been a boy; now he was a man. It didn't seem possible, but Tim was twenty-four now—two years and two days older than Marla. Those years of going together they celebrated their birthdays together, the day after his and the day before hers. Good celebrations, the two years they had the big parties with half the kids in town; and even better, the year they celebrated quietly by themselves.

Marla could see the maturity in the lines in his face, but somehow yesterday's youth was there as well, softening the marks of growing up. Tim's eyes still twinkled as though he were laughing at a private joke. That constant amusement at the world had always bothered Marla's father. More than once he had cautioned her:

"That boy will bring you grief, mark my words."

But when the grief came, he didn't rub it in. For that, Marla would always be thankful.

"Tickets! Tickets, please!"

The conductor was working his way from the back of the train. Marla dug into her purse for the remaining half of her ticket. The pasteboard was ragged along the perforation; the stationmaster at Lyons Falls had said it was the first ticket he could remember selling to Beechhaven.

The conductor took her ticket, then punched a long narrow check, which he stuck beneath Tim's in the slot on the seat before her. Marla could read the legend on the back: "Please carry this check with you whenever leaving your seat."

14

However, she had no intention of leaving her seat before Beechhaven. Her feet ached from her new shoes, and she bent to work them off, sighing in relief as she rubbed the soles of her feet and smoothed a wrinkle in her nylons. A critical eye ran over the stockings; there were no runs in them yet, although she had worn them often enough. Seven unworn pairs remained of the dozen she had received as a Christmas gift last winter. They'd have to last until the end of the war.

As Marla rubbed a toe, she wondered how long that would be—not more than another year, certainly. She couldn't stand more than another year of war.

"Beechhaven?"

"What?" Tim had spoken softly and Marla was unsure of his words. "I'm sorry. Tim; what did you say?"

"Nothing important." The smile came back, but for an instant something else was in his eyes. Something . . . unpleasant? "How's your father, Marla?"

"Not good." She sighed, feeling old, and once more leaned back. "In fact, very poor, Tim. Dr. Vadney says he can't last much longer."

Tim was shocked. "What happened?"

Marla shrugged. "A stroke, we think. You know Dad. He took to bed for a few days and wouldn't let me call the doctor. As soon as he felt better he went back to the yard, and a month later he had a second stroke. Then a heart attack stopped him for good. That was two years ago. He hasn't been able to work since."

"I'm sorry, Marla. Your father always was

15

stubborn as a mule. What about the lumberyard?"

"I quit college to run the office, and Charley Jefferson took care of the yard and the sawmill."

"Old Charley? God, I thought he was dead. He must be ninety if he's a day."

"Eighty at least, though he won't admit it. He can still do the work of a man twenty years younger. But in February we had to throw in the towel. I declared bankruptcy. Dad's worst stroke came right after that."

Tim shook his head. "I don't understand. Your father has a fine reputation. With a working sawmill and the war boom demand for lumber, you should have had more orders than you could handle."

"Priorities," Marla said listlessly. "We couldn't get them—I don't know why. Other people seem to be doing all right. Charley got us one order for fifty thousand line stakes for the new air base they're building at Rome, but that was only because one of Lane's construction superintendents was an old friend."

Tim took Marla's hand and held it gently between his own.

"What about your own lumber?"

"The planer broke down just before Christmas, and I couldn't find new parts, so all we could do was rough finish stuff. The independents started taking their logs elsewhere—said they could get better prices. No logs, no sawmill. No sawmill, no lumberyard."

Tim showed his anger. "That really stinks! Profiteers are cleaning up over this war, while an honestly run small company is thrown to the wolves. I wish I had known, Marla."

"Why? What could you have done?"

"Maybe nothing—I don't know. But I'd certainly have kicked a few butts."

"Well, it's over now." Marla forced a smile. "It isn't the end of the world, Tim—I have a job for the summer, a good one, paying better than anything I could get at the air base or the defense plants. I only wish I didn't have to leave Dad."

"Who's taking care of him?"

"Mrs. Lindner. She has him at her house."

Marla's voice trailed off and she pulled her hand from his grasp, folding it with the other in her lap. For a moment she stared vacantly at the seat before her, then her eyes closed again. She'd had precious little sleep the past few nights, and she could no longer remember the last time she had gone to bed unworried, to sleep a full night through and wake to a day not filled with disaster.

"Your job is at Beechhaven?"

"What?"

Marla opened her eyes to see Tim studying her. The glint of amusement was gone, and a tiny muscle in his jaw was twitching. At this moment he seemed a stranger, and his expression was frightening. She felt a shiver run down her spine. . . .

Two

The hard glare in Tim's eyes faded but did not soften as he asked:

"What's at Beechhaven? I saw your ticket," he added, in a more normal tone.

Marla relaxed, certain that she had mistaken his expression. "You've heard of Garman Gibson?"

He stared blankly for a few seconds, then nodded. "Big-shot. From New York."

"I'm to tutor his two children. I understand they're hellcats, but I suppose it's as close to teaching as I'll ever get, now."

Now . . .

Marla's hands tightened about her purse, the corner of the letter digging into her palm. She didn't have to take it out to remember what it said; after fifty readings, the words were graven in her memory:

. . . At present my wife's illness keeps her confined to her room, and I am unable to give the children the time and attention they need—more so than ever, now that we've lost most of the staff to the war. I'm afraid we'll all be roughing it a bit this summer.

18

If matters work out to our mutual satisfaction, Miss Doren, I feel safe in telling you the position may well become permanent. Of course, your relationship with the children will be the determining factor, their happiness and well-being my only concern. We always return to New York after Labor Day, and the regular position of governess will be open then.

You will find Skelly and Corliss to be good children, exceptionally bright, although I'm afraid they've gone a bit wild since their mother's confinement, and Miss Hurst's return to England. But I'm sure you'll quickly adapt to each other....

The letter was penned in a rough masculine hand, and some words were hard to make out, as though Garman Gibson rarely found it necessary to do his own correspondence. The meaning was clear enough, however, and the job seemed to offer Marla everything she needed most. In the mountains, she could rest.

The letter had come nine days ago and Marla had telegraphed her acceptance immediately. She hurried to wind up the affairs of the lumberyard, the hectic pace not slowing until last night; only then had she been able to turn her attention to packing, trying in one evening to decide on her needs for the next two months.

A chance to rest . . .

She sighed, remembering her last conversation with Dr. Vadney. He'd warned her that she was approaching the breakdown point. Marla had filed applications with most of the defense plants in the area, but the thought of riding forty or fifty miles each way to work, in a car jammed with other war workers, was more than she could bear. And defense-plant work would require a great deal of overtime—ten or twelve hours a day, six days a week. After the strain of the past year, such a schedule would bring a stroke of her own. Summer at Beechhaven would seem more a vacation than a job.

If only she didn't have to leave Dad ...

"For-*rest*-port! Station is Forestport!"

Marla jumped and quickly looked around as the brakeman called out the station. Still half asleep, for a moment she didn't remember where she was. Then she saw Tim looming over her, smiling.

"It's just a stop, Marla. Go back to sleep."

"Oh." Her eyes closed.

The train began to move, swinging into forest as it climbed the broad slope into the mountains. White pine, fir, hemlock, and spruce marched along the ridge spines, while in the lower meadows there were stands of white-trunked poplar, oak, and maple, and an occasional brooding butternut.

Tim rubbed his bristle-covered jaw, shaking his head to stay awake. There were glimpses of water through the forest, for the most part small ponds. For a time the sun was hidden by the crowns of the evergreens crowding close to the train. Even when the sun rose above the timber line the air seemed cooler, the breeze through the open windows evaporating perspiration and helping the weary passengers feel more human.

Without opening her eyes, Marla shifted her

feet, cocking one on the suitcase. The regular rhythm of the wheels over the rail joints was lulling, almost soothing. Weary, Tim hung one arm across the back of her seat, the other resting against the back of the seat before him. Several times he caught himself on the point of dozing and had to regain his balance.

The train passed through the hamlets of Woodgate, Otter Lake, and McKeever; their stations were only shelters beside the tracks. Then steam hissed and brakes clashed as the brakeman came into the car to call, "Thend*ara*!"

The lumberjack woke with a start and stood to stretch and scratch. Marla opened her eyes briefly as he stepped over her; his wool trousers rubbed against her legs, and she checked quickly for a run. Once the remaining nylons were gone, there were still a few pair of silk stockings, far more fragile. When they went, it would be rayon at best, cotton at worst.

Marla was asleep again before Tim could take the seat vacated by the lumberjack. She didn't know when the train moved again and never heard the brakeman announce Eagle Bay, Inlet, and Racquet Lake. It was not until Tim shook her that she woke, startled.

"Wha'—"

"*Beeeeeeech*haven! Station is *Beech*-haven!"

Towering first-growth forest rose above either side of the slowing train, timber that would never know the ax. The sun seemed shut out of this world. As the brakes squealed, the steel rails creaking and groaning in protest, Marla shook her head, trying to clear out the cobwebs, and rubbed her eyes.

21

"Oh, was I ever asleep!"

As the train slowed to a crawl, Tim stood and struggled with her large bag. Marla looked out the window but could see nothing but the forest pushing close. Turning the other way, she saw a small clearing. In it was a shelter, more elaborate than most seen along mountain stops; it was a building rather than a lean-to.

She fumbled for her shoes, wincing and then gasping as she forced her feet into them. Marla stood when the train finally stopped, and saw a man waiting beside a grapple post at the corner of the shelter. He was holding the limp mail sack that had been tossed to him by the train crew, and he seemed to be searching the cars.

Marla could feel the patterns of the upholstery imprinted on the backs of her thighs as she gathered her belongings and smoothed her rumpled clothing, while Tim caught up the other bag. The brakeman was ready with his stool, but Tim jumped from the step before he could drop it, setting the bags down and turning to help Marla. There was no platform—only the gravel of the roadbed, raked smooth. As Marla accepted his hand, she saw a horse standing behind the shelter, the traces of a wagon visible along its flank.

The conductor waved at the locomotive as the brakeman picked up his stool and jumped aboard. The whistle sounded and the train began to move as Tim picked up the suitcases and carried them toward the waiting man.

"Tim!"

He glanced back. "What?"

"The train, you idiot!"

"So?" He grinned. "Let it go—this is where I get off."

Still befuddled with sleep, Marla stared as Tim handed her bags to the waiting man, who tossed the mailbag over his shoulder before accepting the new burden.

"Put Miss Doren's things in the wagon, Davis."

"Yessir, Mr. Layard. I come to collect her." He paused. "Mr. Garman didn't say you was comin'."

"Didn't know myself, till last night. I tried to call but couldn't get a line through."

"Phone's been out since Sunday."

Davis had been eyeing Marla without looking directly at her, and his curiosity made him seem sly. In return, she noted his paint-spattered bib overalls, his well-washed blue workshirts, the sleeves of which were rolled down and buttoned over his knobby wrists, and his battered, shapeless hat. He could have been any age between forty and seventy.

Tim ran his hand through his disordered hair and took advantage of the moment to stretch, doubling his fists and working them into the small of his back. Then he sighed in relief.

"What's the weather forecast, Davis?"

The servant shrugged. "Heavy skies."

Marla glanced skyward; there wasn't a sign of clouds. But the strange discussion continued.

"Any relief from the dowager queen?"

"She ain't reached boil-over yet, but it oughter be comin' soon. Liz is about t' fly."

"Tim!"

Marla's temper was rising to the explosion point, no matter what the unknown dowager queen chose to do. She had spoken angrily, and

Tim read the danger signs. He swallowed the start of another grin.

"What are you doing here?" she demanded.

"I'm sorry, Marla. I should have told you—I work for Gibson Industries International, but these days Garman takes most of my services."

Her fingers trembled against her leg, purse and jacket clutched protectively in her other arm. She could feel her ears burning.

"How long?"

"Have I worked for Garman?" he finished. "About eighteen months—no; twenty."

"Why didn't you tell me? Were you trying to play me for a fool?"

"I'm sorry, Marla—I wanted to surprise you, after I saw your ticket. Forgive me?"

Now he was the little boy caught with his hand in the cookie jar, a pose she remembered too well. Marla bit her lip, trying to hold on to her anger against the urge to melt before his charms as the old angelic expression softened the angular features of the adult Tim. But she knew she was losing the battle.

"Did you know I was coming?"

"No—I was surprised when I saw your ticket. Oh, I knew Garman was looking for a summer tutor, but I have nothing to do with the family."

"What are you doing here?"

"I go where Garman goes. I just finished an errand in New York and came up to Beechhaven to beat the heat. With luck, I should be able to stay over the Fourth."

Marla shook her head, uncertain of her emotions, as the train disappeared around a distant curve, the engineer sounding his whistle a final time. She glanced around at the mournful sound, and saw two large metal storage tanks by a private siding on the far side of the tracks. The gravel and ballast were raked smooth to the level of the tracks, permitting a vehicle to back up to the filler hoses. Red letters on each tank warned INFLAMMABLE, but black labels were nearly obscured by soot from passing trains. From the size of the words, one must be *oil*, the other *gasoline*.

She sighed, conscious of her burning feet, and wanted to slip off her shoes and stockings and wiggle her bare toes in the cool mountain air. Only the sharp-edged gravel stopped her.

Davis kept moving toward the wagon while Marla confronted Tim, who now shamefacedly took her arm. At first she shrugged away, then accepted the gesture, moving against him in her tiredness as though leaning on Tim was something she did every time they were together. Her eyes closed, and for a moment it was as though the last four years had never happened. She didn't see the half-smile curving the corner of his mouth, nor know when it vanished again, worry lines deepening across his brow.

His fingers dug briefly into her arm as she opened her eyes, advancing a half-dozen paces with only his guidance. Then she swallowed, astonished.

"Ye gods! Is there a circus in town?"

Tim laughed, and Marla pulled away, suddenly conscious of his touch—remembering that this was not 1938. More than fourteen hundred days had passed since their last intimacy. Embarrassed, she tried to forget how comfortable it was

25

to be in his arms. She spoke rapidly, staring at the colorful wagon behind the shelter.

"What *is* it?"

"The *Queen of the Lakes*," said Tim. "A hotel wagon."

Marla moved closer, fascinated. The vehicle was unlike any in her experience.

"It's like something from *The Wizard of Oz*!"

"Or a Technicolor nightmare," agreed Tim.

Long and narrow, it was built something like a farmer's work wagon, but much lighter in construction. Two long narrow seats faced each other along the length of the wagonbed, bench and back supports upholstered in rich, dark, buttoned leather. A more conventional board seat for the driver was padded as well, although not as luxuriously as the passenger accommodations.

"All of the big hotels had rigs like this twenty years ago," said Tim, "although I don't think there're any left now in service."

"Was Beechhaven a hotel?"

"It has enough rooms, but no; Garman's grandfather built it as a summer cottage—that was Gabriel. Garman's father, Goulding, collected horse-drawn American vehicles, along with just about anything else a salesman could sucker him into buying."

Marla walked around the wagon, following the explosion of bright colors. A fringed scarlet top sheltered the passengers from the sun, while scarlet curtains were rolled tight, except for one hanging just far enough to reveal the bottom of a purple isinglass window.

Every visible surface of the wagon was decorated, the near sideboard painted with angels frolicking over clouds. The angels were red-cheeked and suspiciously buxom for creatures supposed to be asexual, but their hair was properly angelic gold, their wings and robes pure white.

"It's . . . beautiful. I think."

Tim laughed as Marla looked around and saw Davis loading her suitcases into a box behind the driver's seat. The servant seemed to feel the touch of her eyes against his back; he froze, small bag suspended, for no more than a second, then went on with what he was doing. Marla realized that he was holding himself in tight rein.

No. She shook her head, feeling foolish. You're imagining things, Marla! Davis isn't afraid of you!

She chased away the sudden disturbing thought, and blinked as she glanced at Tim "Are there any other surprises waiting?"

"Beechhaven is loaded with surprises," he said dryly.

"What else? Tell me!"

He shrugged. "You'll know soon enough."

"Oh, tell me, Tim! You know I can't stand surprises."

Changing the subject, Tim said, "Most of Goulding's collections went to the Smithsonian, but he kept out some of his favorite wagons to use up here. There are no roads into the Adirondack Preserve, you know—only the railroad."

Marla glanced at the storage tanks. "Then why—"

"The gas is for the electric generators and the oil is for a burner in the servants' quarters over the boathouse. There's precious little of either left. We're using kerosene lamps while Garman tries to wangle priorities. The fireplaces are for chilly evenings, and the gas range is for cooking."

"There's hot water, I hope."

"Pea-coal heaters in each bathroom. There's plenty of that, at least."

Marla traced a finger over the gilt work, then snatched it away, feeling like a small child. The wagon box was a wine red, the running gear and spokes a bright yellow. Every possible surface was filled with tracery and scrollwork.

"It is beautiful," she decided.

"It's the showpiece of the collection—what's left of it. The catalog has color plates of several eighteenth-century carriages that were outstanding—one belonged to Marie Antoinette."

Marla sighed, envying the lifestyle that permitted such extravagance. Except for bits of forest dust and leaf mold clinging to the iron-shod wheels, the wagon was spotless.

"How old is it?"

"Sixty or seventy years," said Tim. "I understand Goulding found it a wreck in a leaking stable. He put his team of restorers on it for four years."

"Team?"

"Old-timers who worked in a carriage factory that he closed down about 1915. He kept them busy right up till the day he died, six years ago."

Davis was in the box, hands grasping the reins, head sunk down into his shoulders. The horse snorted, tossing its head, and Tim moved to stroke the gray's neck.

"No sugar this time, Major. Sorry."

Davis made an impolite noise but didn't turn around. Marla followed Tim to the back of the wagon and took his hand as she mounted the single iron step. The step and its supports were wrought to resemble climbing vines.

The wagon creaked beneath her weight and settled toward one corner, until Tim followed and sat opposite her. Their knees almost touched in the close space.

"It seems rather overdoing it, this conveyance for just two people—one, since you weren't expected."

"Don't let Davis fool you," said Tim. "He's proud of the *Queen*. Otherwise he'd have brought the buggy."

Davis clucked his tongue twice at that, then yanked on the reins, and Major backed a few paces to his urging. One more flick of the reins started Major forward, unseen small bells jingling. The siding was long enough for half a dozen cars, but the clearing narrowed rapidly as they left the tracks. In less than fifty yards they were beneath the trees, the temperature dropping several degrees more. Marla sighed as the sun left her face, and twisted around to put her feet up on the other seat, only inches from Tim. She still felt sticky, but the movement of the wagon created a small breeze.

"How far is the house?"

"Nearly a mile."

Tim slumped down, cocking one foot on the other seat and easing himself to where his arm fell along the back rest. His other hand fell to his thigh, separated from Marla's leg by no more than a few inches. She noticed, face burning, but he made no further advance.

Marla's eyes touched his, flicked away, then moved back when Tim closed his own. What had she thought he was going to do? The question went unanswered, but she knew that briefly she had been afraid.

But of Tim? Or herself?

The dirt road stretched deep into the woods, a cool tunnel that seemed impenetrable when she glanced ahead. Thin poles were spaced evenly along the grassy shoulder, each supporting a single glass transformer and carrying one strand of wire. When Tim opened his eyes a few minutes later, he confirmed that the line was the telephone.

"When it works. Which is less often than not. I'm afraid you'll find Beechhaven . . . isolated, Marla."

She tried to read the deeper meaning in his words as he lapsed into silence again, and fought her own urge to doze off. Marla knew that Tim had been about to say something else but had changed his mind at the last instant. It was an old habit, one that had always annoyed her. But there was no point in pressing him; whatever he had been about to say, he would tell her in his own good time.

She studied his face, until something cold passed over the back of her neck, and she shivered. Even though Tim's eyes were closed she imagined that he was staring at her. It was like looking into a bottomless pool.

Then he opened his eyes again and blinked rapidly. He grinned, and years fell away.

"I'm glad you're here, Marla. I've missed you."

Marla sat up, drawing her knees away from him as a lump grew in her chest. Despite the sudden announcement, this was not the Tim Layard she remembered . . . not the youth she had loved.

(Still loved?) The lump was sharp-edged, hurting; but the question was unanswerable.

She forced a question: "Do you come here often?"

"I go where Garman sends me. I'll probably be on the move most of the summer, but I should get back for a day or two every couple weeks."

He yawned, covering his mouth. "Right at the moment, dynamite wouldn't move me. All I want is to fall into bed and sleep for twenty-four hours."

Marla shook her head. "First I want the hottest bath in the world."

"I wouldn't dare—I'd fall asleep in the tub and drown." Again the grin. "Unless you need me to scrub your back?"

Marla flushed. Four years had certainly made him bolder. Before she could retort, the wagon wheels bounced over a stone and she was thrown forward, her knee banging into his leg. Tim caught her, then quickly released her.

"Are you okay?"

"Yes." She looked away, flustered. "I . . . I've never met Mr. Gibson. What's he like? What are the children like?"

"Wild, I suppose," he said, answering the second question. "But it's not their fault. You'll get along with Corliss and Skelly. It's their mother and grandmother you'll have to worry about."

"Bethel—Mrs. Gibson?"

"The young Mrs. Gibson. Alicia is *the* Mrs. Gibson, and don't you forget it."

Marla was wide awake now. The strong scent of forest evergreens filled the air, which, except for the creaking of the wagon and the soft plodding of Major's hooves in the leaf mold, was summer somnolent. The sun was screened out of this stretch, the road lost in eternal twilight.

"Bethel is the children's mother?"

"Garman's wife, yes. Whatever you say to her, don't mention the war. She takes it as a personal affront."

Marla smiled, then sobered. "But she is sick?"

"Bethel's best role is playing the invalid. She was born two generations after her time."

"Tell me more about Alicia. She sounds frightening."

"Alicia has the staff terrified—what's left of it; she runs Beechhaven with an iron hand. Between Bethel's whining and Alicia's demands, it's a wonder any servants remain. In her favor is the fact that she never descends from her glass tower—but expect a summons to inspection the minute you set foot on the porch."

Marla glanced at the wreckage of her traveling clothes. "Like this?" she asked, dismayed.

"Appearances won't matter—Alicia will have a low opinion of you even if you look as though you stepped from the pages of *Harper's Bazaar.*"

"Can't I have my bath first?"

"Only if you run down to the dock and jump in the lake. Which behavior would have you on the next train south."

Marla sighed. "I suppose everything is by time-table."

"Dinner at seven, children in bed at eight-thirty, servants in bed at ten. Everyone in the house is afraid of Alicia. Even Garman."

"And you?"

"I avoid confrontations, but I'm sure Alicia has a low opinion of me, for no other reason than the fact I work for a living."

"She sounds formidable."

"And dangerous."

Tim changed position, stretched, and settled again. "I better warn you, Marla—there's a strong practical-joker streak in the Gibson family. Look at everything twice—not for tacks; they've advanced beyond that. Just watch your step."

Marla's eyes widened as she glanced toward Davis. Tim nodded approvingly. "Davis is one person you can trust. He sees everything that happens, and probably knows where the bodies are buried, but he keeps his mouth shut."

The servant gave no sign of hearing. After ten seconds Marla looked back to Tim.

"Tell me more about the children."

Tim shrugged, rubbing his chin, the rasp of stubble momentarily louder than the creaking of the wagon. He blinked, and when his hand dropped, his face was without expression. Their eyes touched, and Marla felt another chill run down her spine.

"Is something the matter?" she asked, faltering.

Before Tim answered, the forest fell away from the road as the wagon crested a steep knoll.

Major hesitated a moment, then lurched forward, the sudden movement throwing Marla to the side. She caught herself with her left hand, and looked ahead to Beechhaven.

Three

The house sprawled over the broad top of another knoll, squat in its immensity, still a quarter mile way. Despite incongruent protrusions and spires, and sunlight reflecting off scores of windows, the red mass reminded Marla of an armory, a windowless fortress. Fingers of trees reached cautiously toward the lawns, but before the wagon dropped down the slope she saw the glint of steel-blue water in the distance.

Marla caught her breath. "Oh, my!"

Tim laughed. "You're not dreaming."

The lawns dropped away to left and right, flower beds ranked in regular rows a measured hundred feet from the house. To the rear, the explosion of color was broken only where the road cut through a succession of tulips, each color segregated to its own bed. A dozen chimneys broke the skyline, wisps of smoke rising lazily from one to feather into nothingness against the pale sky.

Marla gnawed at a knuckle, trying to take in every detail. A white animal broke over the slope, ambling slowly toward the flower beds and followed a moment later by two or three more.

"Sheep?" she asked, beyond amazement.

"Garman had them sent up from his farm near Pauling," explained Tim. "They're a little smelly in close quarters, but they do a good job on the grass, so long as you keep them moving. Let them stay in one spot and they'll crop it to the ground."

"How many rooms does it have?"

Tim shrugged. "Fifty, a hundred—the plumber says there're fourteen bathrooms. The kids claim even their grandfather never kept track, although Goulding constantly made changes to Gabriel's original plans. I'm told the carpenters were here all season long every year while Goulding was alive."

Marla caught a note of bitterness in his voice, but when she looked, his expression was blank. His eyes were sunken, revealing his exhaustion, and she wondered if her own appearance was as bad.

"It must take an army of servants."

"Eighteen, last year. I understand there were more in the old days. This summer the family is hurting; they're trying to get by with only a skeleton staff—no laundress, for one. It goes out three times a week to a woman in Racquet Lake And no personal maids, although Alicia and Bethel run the girls they do have ragged."

Davis made a noise, but when Marla glanced toward him his expression seemed no different. She looked ahead again.

"The grounds are beautiful."

"The head gardener came back—he had three helpers two years ago, one last year. None this year. He's a Filipino, keeps threatening to join the army, 'fight for MacArthur.' Garman thinks he's too old, but nobody can find out his age."

"He must be a genius, judging from the flower beds."

"Corliss claims Rubio is half-plant himself. He appeared years ago, from nowhere, and started working without being hired. Every winter he vanishes with the first snow, but come April he's back."

"The staff must have a terrible time without electricity. How many other servants are there?"

"Things have slipped," said Tim. "It's a good thing Bethel took to her room this year—Alicia never comes down anyway. Davis and his wife run the house—Liz is saddled with the cooking as well this year. They stay here year round and keep the roofs clear of snow during the winter. How many girls this week, Davis?"

"Three," said the driver. "That Angie quit, but two new ones showed up Monday. Sisters."

"Garman find a boatman yet?"

"Nope."

"Cassini must be screaming," said Tim; then he explained, "He's the stable master."

"Dumps it on the kid," said Davis.

"That's understandable," said Tim. "Cassini is not one of my favorite people, Marla."

"Good with the horses," said Davis, flatly.

"And Bethel's pet," added Tim. "Any guests this week?"

"Just that French feller. Mr. Garman's expectin' three or four more tonight, comin' up on the private car."

"Philippe doesn't count. He's been here all season."

Marla shook her head. "Eight servants doesn't seem very many for a place this size."

"Eighteen wasn't enough last year," said Tim. "I've seen thirty sleeping over, in addition to the family. No big weekends this year, though. Thank God. Or thank Bethel's confinement."

The wagon rolled through a corridor of young elms, then started uphill again, the house looming above them. Half a dozen buildings were clustered between the two knolls, hidden among the trees and screened from the house. There were windows open to reveal half a dozen vehicles, including a red-painted tank wagon.

Then the stable, announcing itself with a mound of manure heaped on the side away from the house. Marla heard the snort of a horse and then another answered, Major tossing his head.

A long, open shed was attached to the far side of the stable, half filled with cordwood. Then they were out of the trees and crossing the bordering flowers, protected from the grazing sheep by staked wire fencing. The road climbed sharply, then angled in a circle that hugged the house, gray cinders crunching beneath the iron wheels of the wagon.

Now Marla saw that the house was girdled by a screened porch that made a sudden dip almost to ground level as it rounded the south corner. It continued for a third of the length of the building, which was nearly two hundred feet. Then the porch jumped to what must be the third story, steps zigzagging thirty feet, then dropped almost to the original level, perhaps three or four feet higher, to finish the run to the north corner.

Tim saw Marla twisting her head to stare up at the high stretch. "Gabriel's bedroom—he wanted his own private entrance. Why, I don't know. There's no other room on that corridor."

For a moment Marla couldn't remember which was Gabriel, Garman's father or grandfather. So many *g*s were confusing. A family tradition? No; Skelly was Garman's only son.

Gabriel was Garman's grandfather. In her weariness she felt satisfied to have them sorted out.

"Seems a strange location," she said. "If this were my house, I'd want a view of the lake."

"Gabriel built Beechhaven for his wife, but to the dictates of his own amusement. I understand she refused to set foot inside once she saw what he'd done—wouldn't even come down the hill. She made Gabriel drive her back to their private car, where she stayed until he arranged for a train to take her out."

Good for her, thought Marla. Even without knowing her, she admired that sort of independence.

The roof was slate, the house covered with cedar shakes for siding, in places painted, in others left to weather to a natural gray-brown. Some of the painted sections seemed heavily weathered as well. As her eyes passed over the house, she could see neither rhyme nor reason to the disparate elements; it looked as though an enthusiastic child had built a cake of uneven and lopsided layers. She could see three chimneys, each of different style and material. Everywhere eaves and gables and the cornice of the porch were encrusted with Victorian gingerbread, adjoining sections sometimes painted in clashing colors.

There was too much to take in; then Marla gasped.

"One of the children is on the roof!"

"Where?"

Tim twisted, following her pointing finger to a figure crouching in the shadows between a gable and a chimney. Marla blinked; she was sure that the child had shrunk back. Then Tim laughed.

"Look over there, Marla—behind the ventilator."

She obeyed, and saw another crouching figure, squat and seemingly malformed. Neither Garman nor Tim had said anything about the children being abnormal!

"They'll get hurt!"

"It's not the kids—just a couple of the kings. Henrys VII and XIII, I think—I never can keep them straight. There, over on the corner: that's George I. Have you ever seen green children?"

Marla, squinting against the sun glare, made out the indicated figure. Out of the shadows, it was gray-green and seemed not to move.

"A gargoyle?" she asked, deflated.

"Technically, no. Gargoyles are rainspouts— the kings are just bogeys. You'll find them everywhere—animals, people, dozens of them, in the damnedest places, inside and out. The kids can introduce you—they've given them all names."

Marla sighed. "What else—secret panels?"

"Certainly. Secret rooms, too. Watch your step: fall through the wrong wall and you could wander for days before anyone found you."

Marla was certain that he was kidding; then she let her eyes pass across the house again, and was sure of nothing.

The wagon made the sharp turn around the northeast corner, and she looked toward the lake—and her eyes were caught by the tower seeming to grow out of the front of the house.

She swallowed, cutting off the exclamation. The base of the tower started at midlevel, reaching out at least twenty feet and buttressed by shingled supports. From there, the walls seeming solid glass, it soared up another two stories, which carried it well above the general roofline, pulling that corner of the house off-balance until it seemed in danger of slipping down the slope. The tower was roofed by a red-painted coolie's cap that reminded her of the stovepipe protectors over the train depots.

Although the sun was over the far side of the house, it spilled through the tower, the light gathered into a blinding mirror. Marla blinked, then closed her eyes against red spots and turned her head away. When she opened them again, the wagon had moved far enough for the mirror effect to be thrown off-center.

"Alicia's lair?" she asked.

Tim nodded, "None other."

It was impossible to see inside those glass walls, but as Marla let her eyes move up again she had the disturbing feeling that someone was watching. She forced her eyes down again and glanced at the porch, which ran just above them now. It was screened along the entire length, but it seemed narrower than it had across the rear of the house.

'The whole place needs painting," she said, for need of something to say. She would not look up at the tower again.

"Find the painters," said Tim, "and Garman will give you a bonus."

The tower was overhead, roofing the drive as it rounded the front of the house. More broad lawns swept down to the lake, two hundred yards away. A boathouse bulked along the shore, at least fifty feet long and two stories high; she remembered that it housed the servants' quarters. A long narrow dock on the north poked a hundred feet or more out into the lake, two or three small boats tied to it. A hundred yards out was anchored a raft with a diving board.

The lake itself stretched two or three miles into the distance, while the house overlooked a narrow cove. A heavily forested island, or a finger of the far shore, poked within a thousand yards of the cove.

Davis brought the wagon under a porte cochere that guarded the center of the house, the porch screening stopping twenty feet short of the broad double doors of the main entrance. Tall, skinny windowlights only a few inches wide, covered by lace curtains, guarded either side of the doors. The unscreened section was empty, although Marla spotted at least two porch swings and a dozen rattan chairs in the protected portions.

Davis stepped across to the platform, then turned back for her bags. Tim stretched some of the weariness from his back as he stood, then dropped to the ground, turning to offer his hand to Marla. Before she could set both feet on the cindered drive, the doors exploded open and two whirlwinds burst out of the house.

"Tim! You didn't say you were coming back so soon!"

Corliss shouted the greeting, skidding to a stop with her brother half a pace back. Their eyes studied Marla as Tim returned their waves and gave the same brief explanation he had given Davis. Self-conscious, Marla started to tug at her skirt, then stopped, with one hand suspended. Seconds dragged, and then she followed Tim as he mounted the near set of steps to the porch. He placed a hand on each child's head, ruffling their hair.

"Outlaws, meet Miss Doren—your keeper for the summer. She doesn't look it, but behind that mild exterior she's worse than your grandmother."

Marla's ears burned as Corliss laughed. Skelly only stared, eyes big but face expressionless. Marla looked away, trying to break the spell, and then studied them from the corners of her eyes.

Corliss was the girl, of course: twelve years old. Skelly was a year younger. Both were nut brown, with blond hair bleached almost white. There certainly hadn't been time to build a tan like that this summer. Then she remembered that they had wintered in Florida.

Brother and sister were dressed in similar polo shirts with bright horizontal stripes and short brown pants, and both were barefoot. The family relationship was unmistakable, although Skelly's face was still round with baby fat. Corliss was as angular as any boy, but the sharp observer could pick out the first signs of womanhood. By the end of summer there would be visible changes.

Now the girl wore pigtails that pulled her hair tight. If not for them, she could have been

Skelly's elder brother. Bright blue eyes stared from both young faces.

"Hello," said Marla, lamely. She was saved from floundering when the door opened again and Garman Gibson came out. He strode purposefully across the broad porch, hand out in greeting.

"You must be Miss Doren. Welcome to Beechhaven—I'm Garman Gibson." Aside, he added, "Hello, Tim. I didn't know you were back."

Marla swallowed as her hand rose slowly, attracted to the magnet that was her employer's physical power. His masculine warmth enfolded her, coursing through his smile and transmitted through the electric touch of his hand—not in normal fashion. Instead, he clasped her cross-palm and held her, exerting a small measure of strength. A shock crossed her spine.

"Welcome," he said again.

"Thank you." Marla realized she was bobbing her head. Tim was good-looking if not actually handsome, but Garman Gibson was the most handsome man she had ever seen, his physical presence enough to take her breath.

She studied him until she realized she was staring, and then broke the eye lock with a tiny shudder that she hoped went unnoticed. There was something of Robert Taylor in his face and in the way he carried himself, yet his power outshone that of any movie star. He seemed out-of-place in the mountain setting, dressed in a summerweight suit of tan silk, jacket open to show vest and a contrasting small-figured brown silk tie. The tailoring was impeccable, his shoes buffed to a gleaming gloss, his nails manicured. Her eyes touched his fingers again, and she was sure he wore colorless nail polish.

The dandified touch broke the spell. Garman was two or three inches shorter than Tim, but even standing close he seemed taller . . . self-assurance, she decided. Garman Gibson knew he was rich and he accepted his position. More important, he was aware of the power that came with that position.

But he was a fop. He was still holding her hand while Tim repeated for the third time his explanation of his unexpected reappearance. Garman said something in response, his voice low and throaty—he must have practiced the tone, trying to imitate Clark Gable.

Good heavens, Marla, you can tell he's posing! Stop acting like a giddy schoolgirl!

"You've met the children," said Garman, "and my mother is waiting. I'll take you to her."

"Oh!" She glanced down at the wreckage of her traveling clothes, remembering Tim's warning—and decided to make a stand for independence. "I really must wash up first."

Garman blinked, the cloak of self-assurance slipped, cracking the shell. Marla saw doubt in his eyes, and firmed her own resolve, locking stares again. Defeated, his voice rose half a tone.

"Please don't be long. Davis, take Miss Doren's things to Blue South. And tell Mrs. Davis that Mother says the salmon salad for lunch, not the ham."

He started to turn, uncertain of his next move now that Marla had revised the script. She glanced at Tim—to see the same expression she had caught earlier freezing his features. A jaw muscle twitched, and his teeth were clenched tight; then the expression dissolved in a smoothered yawn as he covered his mouth, and she was no longer sure. . . .

Tim couldn't be filled with hatred.

"Tim, I'll see you in the office in five minutes."

During the introductions, Davis had stood, mailbag over his shoulder, Marla's suitcases in his hands. Now he set them down long enough to give the mailbag to Garman, who quickly stripped the leather strap and pulled out a sheaf of letters. He bent them to slip off the binding string and leafed through, obviously not finding what he expected. He dug into the bag again for a loose assortment of newspapers and magazines, but there was nothing more.

He turned away, Corliss skipping ahead to hold the door for her father. Garman went into the house without comment, the mailbag seeming out-of-place draped over his arm. Davis picked up the suitcases again and followed, Marla and Tim moving together and nearly colliding. He stopped, backed off, and made a sweeping motion with his hand as he bowed.

"After you, m'lady."

Marla tried to smile, but it ended in a jawcracking yawn. She followed Davis into a broad entrance hall gloomy with darkness, the children and Tim crowding on her heels. Her footsteps clacked on polished parquet for three paces before moving onto a broad oriental rug. After the summer warmth, the hall seemed chill, the air carrying a faint mustiness of closed spaces.

She blinked, eyes adjusting to the dimmer light. High overhead, a stained-glass skylight brought in the sun in colored shards that broke against a broad golden oak staircase that mounted in a half-curve to a second-floor landing. A gallery circled the well, which was at least twenty feet across, while smaller twin staircases cut straight from the landing to the third floor.

No marble? Marla was disappointed. A crystal chandelier was suspended from the gallery and there were electric light fixtures along the walls, but several side tables carried kerosene lamps and larger, metal-based and -shaded gas lamps.

To her left, a set of sliding doors stood open. Garman descended the last of three steps into a room crammed with massive furniture. The top of a huge rolltop desk stood open, while massive bookcases and cabinets bulked against the one visible wall. That must be the office, thought Marla.

The staircase was twenty feet from the main entrance, a broad balustrade circling a small alabaster statue at the base: a female nude. There were other statuary scattered around the hall, alternately male and female. As Marla passed the office she looked in and saw three sets of tall, narrow windows in the front wall, their ledges shoulder height. Dark red velvet drapes were caught back and narrow slatted shutters stood open to let in daylight from the porch. Garman dropped the mail onto the desk, picked up the telephone receiver, and jiggled the hook impatiently. Then he slammed down the dead instrument.

Another set of sliding doors led from that side of the hall, but they were closed, so she couldn't see the room beyond. On the far side a single set stood open, one step mounting up into the room revealed. Marla saw a grand piano and massive guardians, but the room was too dim to make out anything more. Against the walls of the hall were heavy pieces, both cabinets and couches, but the entrance was big enough to diminish the furnishings. Between the office and the closed doors was a seven-foot-tall hall rack, her image ghostly in the rippled mirror as she passed.

Marla tried to take in everything, her steps faltering until Skelly and Corliss moved past, hurrying after Davis. She glanced around; Tim had vanished.

"No ballroom?" she asked, amused.

"It's on the second floor," said Corliss, stopping to wait for her. "It isn't used anymore."

"A shame," Marla said wryly.

Corliss prattled on: "When Grandmother married Grandfather, they had a great big chessboard in the middle of the ballroom, and one year they gave a formal ball where servants took the place of the chess pieces for a game. Do you play?"

"Chess? No, I'm afraid not."

"Skelly stinks," said Corliss. "And Tim never has time to give me a game. I'll teach you."

Marla noticed a great highboy chest and several wing chairs brooding from various corners. The hall continued past the staircase, diminished, and dwindled into the shadowy depths. She started up, Corliss at her side, feeling an aching in her legs and once more aware of her burning feet. The landing was at least twenty feet above the main level.

"Are you a good swimmer?" asked Corliss.

"Passable." Marla wondered if the child ever ran down.

"Do you like to dive?"

"Not off the high board. Heights make me nervous."

"Oh." Corliss swung her pigtails. "We don't have a high board here. Do you play tennis?"

Above, Davis had disappeared. Skelly paused at the top of the steps long enough to look down at the laggards; then he ducked to the right, dropping below the railing. Marla caught a glimpse of bright color as he scooted on hands and knees behind the banister, then was gone.

She glanced at Corliss. "Now tennis is my game. Is there a court?"

"Oh sure; we got clay and grass both."

"We *have* clay and grass," Marla corrected. If she was to be tutor, she should get into the habit. "You'll have to give me a game—tomorrow."

"Okay. I'm pretty good—I can beat Tim three out of five sets, and Jack better than that."

"Jack?"

"He helps Mr. Cassini."

Cassini was the stable master; Jack must be his college-boy aide. Despite Tim's description of the workload, the staff obviously found a certain amount of time for play. Which seemed only fair; the private mountain lake looked like it had been designed by God as a playground.

They reached the landing, Marla pausing to lean on the broad rail, sighing as she shifted to equalize the weight on her aching calf muscles. Oh, to be on her way to bed! Even without Tim's warnings, she found herself resenting Alicia Gibson for denying her that immediate relief. It

49

would be easy to sink down right here, rest her cheek against the carved stair post, close her eyes. . . .

She blinked, shaking off the blanket of sleep with an effort, and looked around the landing. The balustrade continued around the well, unbroken, a graceful oval flattened at the stair posts to make stands for more small statues. Marla stood near the center of the gallery, the walls blank on all sides, without doors. The side galleries narrowed as they passed the bottom of the twin staircases, and became little more than a catwalk barely wide enough for one person where it crossed the front of the well. A circular bull's-eye window above the gallery seemed centered over the doors below, the glass giving a distorted view of the lake.

On this end the side galleries dead-ended in alcoves perhaps six feet deep. The one to the left, north, was almost filled by a massive chest of drawers nearly the height of a man. The other alcove held only a pair of backless carpenter's benches facing each other.

Where were Davis and Skelly? She scanned the gallery again, then looked up the smaller staircases to the next landing, although if either had gone that way she would have seen them. Skelly had cut to the right, and now she was sure that Davis had turned that way as well. But the only thing on that wall was a triple rank of photographs in dreary black frames, obscuring the bright French wallpaper painted in eighteenth-century court scenes.

Marla moved that way, leaning her weight on the railing, eyes traveling over the nearest of the photos. Most were severe, family groups that seemed to date from the last century, the women in dresses that swept the ground and the men in stiff collars that sawed their necks. The children were overdressed and scowling with their elders. Most certainly they were not the sort of pictures she would have chosen to decorate a wall—any wall. Such grim reminders of yesterday should be kept in old albums, away from the light of day where they could depress brighter spirits.

Then her glance touched one in the middle rank and half a dozen positions from the end. It was of three boys, two in knickers and caps, the youngest, perhaps six or seven, in a one-piece linen suit with sailor collar. The older boys were laughing, leaning against each other. The Gibson resemblance was unmistakable. The oldest might have been Skelly, but for the clothes, which marked the picture at least a generation earlier.

Compared to its neighbors, the photograph seemed to have captured a happy moment, although the youngest boy's face was blank, the expression again reminding Marla of Skelly. Her eyes rested on the child for a moment, captured by the hypnotic quality of his stare. The longer she looked at him, the stronger was the feeling that he was aware of her presence, was returning her gaze.

You're imagining things! Watch out, or next you'll be seeing ghosts.

She blinked, forcing her eyes away from the photographs. *Where* were Davis and Skelly? They might have dropped through a secret panel . . . perhaps Tim hadn't been kidding.

51

At the moment she did not find the thought amusing.

She sighed. "All right, Corliss, I give up. Where did they go?"

"Wait here."

Smothering a giggle, Corliss moved to the south alcove and walked between the benches—and through the solid wall.

Four

Marla blinked, shook her head, and pressed thumb and forefinger to the sockets of her eyes, rubbing them once to ease the strain of exhaustion. The alcove was the same, but Corliss had disappeared.

She moved closer, fingers trailing the rail, until at last the girl loomed out of the gloom, the wall no longer solid. Behind her, a mirror angled, created the illusion of a solid partition. Now Marla could make out a corridor, the extension of the alcove, running toward the back of the house. As she approached Corliss, the illusion shattered, and in the distance she saw a lace-curtained window, and through it a narrow view of distant treetops.

"Nice," she said dryly.

"Great-grandfather was an amateur magician," explained Corliss, as Marla came close enough to see her own image in the angled mirror.

"What other tricks did he play?"

"Oh, we're not allowed to tell. That would spoil the fun."

Giggling, Corliss turned and skipped ahead, passing several anonymous doors to duck into a cross-corridor. When Marla reached the spot she found herself at the foot of another flight of stairs, enclosed; six steps up, they bent, and then again, doubling back, to come out on another front-to-rear corridor.

She paused to catch her breath, lifting one foot and then the other to ease the aching. The right wall of the staircase continued across the corridor, blinding it, but she eyed it skeptically before leaning her weight against it; nothing happened. Then Corliss popped back into the corridor to see what was keeping her. Push on, Marla—how much farther can it be?

The corridor was short, and there was a single door cut into the right wall. Corliss led her past it, at which point the corridor opened into another, which cut all the way across the back of the house, an open staircase at the north disappearing below.

Corliss turned south. The inside wall of the corridor was blank; the outside one was broken every few feet by windows, each with lace curtains. Marla looked out and saw a foreshortened man far below walking in the flower beds: he must be the gardener. Two of the sheep were visible, dangerously close to the fence guarding the tulips. The gardener suddenly ran at them, waving a stick, and they broke away, but ran only half a dozen paces before stopping to resume their grazing.

Corliss found it difficult to hold herself down to Marla's foot-sore pace, and she turned around several times to back away impatiently. At the end of the hall was a white doorway trimmed in red; a short corridor ran off to the right again. Two more white doors were on the left, and there was a single one to the right only a few feet from the corner.

"Blue South is over here," said Corliss, skipping back to the third door. The color of the trim matched the name. The second door was trimmed in yellow. "That's the bath," she added, indicating the right-hand door. "You don't have to share, at least not yet—Philippe is North. Most guests are North or East."

Who was Philippe? Before Marla could ask, Davis came out of the blue-trimmed door, leaving it open, and paused just short of a collision.

"I lit the gas lamp in the bathroom."

"Oh. Thank you." Why was he looking past her ear? His Adam's apple jumped. "Is there hot water?"

"Built the fire 'fore breakfast."

"Thank you," she said again, feeling the response inadequate.

She moved aside to let him pass, and her eyes followed him until he turned into the back corridor and was gone. She was surprised to feel relief; despite what Tim had said about Davis, something in the man's manner disturbed her.

Corliss ducked into the room; Marla followed, then stopped in the doorway, blinking in astonishment. The room was perhaps twenty feet square. The canopied bed opposite the door was the first thing to catch her eye. It was centered between French windows, which were open, a breeze stirring soft curtains over them. Beyond the windows was a small private porch, circular and screened.

Corliss plopped down on a padded bench, her hands dropping flat, as Marla entered the room.

The girl arched her back over the mattress, pig-tails dropping to brush the navy blue quilted comforter that hung on both sides to the floor.

"I think this is the nicest guest room."

"It's lovely," agreed Marla.

The furniture was old, and several of the pieces were too large for any normal-size room, but they seemed well suited to this chamber. To her right, a cherry chest with a large beveled mirror filled the space between two closets; to Marla's left, just within the room, was a dressing table with another padded bench, the twin of the one at the foot of the bed. Then she looked at Corliss again and saw that her seat was actually a storage chest.

Against the left wall was a double dresser, with a loveseat angled between it and the far window. In the corner by the corridor wall, a chaise lounge pointed out into the room, while diametrically opposite was a wing chair, and in front of that was a platform rocker that almost blocked the rear window. Marble-topped night-stands flanked the bed, the wood shining with rubbing that brought out the grain in attractive highlights.

Apart from the wood furniture, everything in the room was blue; even the rug was fielded in several shades of the primary color, although pale pink cabbage roses added a touch of contrast. The carpet came within a foot of the wall on all sides, and seemed a single large piece. Upholstered pieces were in a blue print pattern, the walls blue wainscoting to the waist and papered above it, pale yellow and white roses against a cloudy blue background. The exposed floorboards were painted the same blue-gray shade as the wainscoting. The skirt of the canopy matched the comforter, and gauzy curtains were a medium blue.

Marla's spirits were lifted by the room. She smiled as her eyes touched Corliss again.

"It's the nicest room I've ever seen."

Corliss cocked her head. "Blue is your color. You'd look ghastly in green."

Marla glanced down at her skirt. "Thanks a lot."

"Oh, a little green's okay," said the girl, sure of herself. "That's a pretty suit. But in one of the green rooms you'd look dead."

The thought was not pleasant. "This is like something out of *American Home* or *House Beautiful.*"

"It was decorated—Mother and her pansy decorator did it. He has yukky taste, but this is one of their few successes. Grandmother says even people without taste have to do something right once in a while, by accident."

The girl's attitude toward her mother surprised Marla almost as much as her casual use of crude language. She started to say something, then thought better of it. Wait until she was on firmer footing before interfering.

Better yet, stay out of family matters entirely. That way could lead only to grief. No matter what Tim said, interfering at this point could be dangerous. Keep your nose clean and tend to your own affairs. The Gibsons were a strange clan and they moved in a different world from Marla's.

Marla sighed, eyeing the bed again; it gave every appearance of comfort. She restrained herself from testing it—once down, it would be impossible to pull herself up again, and she had to face Alicia now.

A soft breeze stirred the curtains and touched her face with a barely felt caress. This was a pleasant room; she could be happy here. It was much the nicest room she had even known—certainly a good many levels above the hand-me-down furniture she had grown up with.

Summer at Beechhaven was going to be comfortable, at least physically. Even if they did have to rough it a bit, if doing without electricity could be called roughing it.

She glanced at the ceiling light fixture; there were two small wall fixtures as well, flanking the door. Perhaps Garman would find his supply of gasoline before the summer was over. For now she'd have to learn to get along with the gas and the kerosene lamps—and be thankful that they weren't reduced to candles. One of the mantled gas lamps stood on one of the nightstands; she'd have to learn how to light it. There was a hurricane lamp as well, on the vanity; at least she could handle that.

Marla completed her examination of the room and turned to Corliss, locking eyes with her as she sat up, hunching forward, with head drawn down between her shoulders. The child's face was suddenly solemn, her pupils unnaturally large, a deep blue that was almost gray. They were compelling in their intensity, reminding Marla of the boy in the photograph.

Corliss tossed her head. "Well?"

"Well what?" returned Marla, suddenly nervous.

"Do you like Beechhaven, Marla?"

The child seemed earnest as she asked the question, and Marla chose her words with care.

"I like what I've seen so far, yes. Tell me, Corliss—what was your governess's name?"

"Miss Hurst. She went back to Scotland to take over her brother's public school so's he could go in the army. Isn't that dumb. Marla? The British call their private schools public, and their public schools private. I think it's silly."

"Americans seem silly to the Britons. What did you call Miss Hurst?"

"Miss Hurst, of course—oh." Her face fell. "You want us to call you Miss Doren."

"Don't you think it would be appropriate?"

Corliss looked away and sighed. "But you're not at all like Miss Hurst."

"In what way?"

"She's ever so old—at least forty. And we call Tim and Jack by their first names."

Get off on the right foot, Marla. You like Corliss, and you'll probably like Skelly, once you get to know him. But you're not here as a playmate for them.

"Jack and Tim aren't responsible for you. I am. Do you see the difference?"

Her eyes continued to wander. "I s'pose so."

"I want us to be friends, Corliss." Marla smiled. "But right now I have to make myself presentable for your grandmother, so if you'll excuse me . . ."

Corliss looked at her briefly, then stood, moving to the door. She paused, hand on the knob, as though she was about to say something more; then she thought better of it, and left, closing the door gently.

Marla sighed, wondering if she had made a mistake. No; you did that exactly right. Be friendly but keep your distance. You have to command their respect, and fraternization is not the way.

She swung her large suitcase onto the padded chest, then had to fumble through her purse for the keys. Opened, she lifted the protector and shook out the two dresses on top. No electricity—how would she get them pressed?

Worry about that later; there must be some alternative. She tossed the dresses across the foot of the bed, too tired to take them to the closet, and rummaged for a fresh skirt and blouse. She slipped out of her bedraggled traveling clothes. The linen suit would have to go to a dry cleaner, perhaps when the laundry went to Racquet Lake. Surveying the wreckage, she hoped the cleaner could salvage it.

Digging her robe out of the other compartment, she sat on the vanity bench to pry off her shoes, massaging her burning feet before tugging the nylons straight; then she donned mules. Flat-heeled shoes were in the bottom of the suitcase; she retrieved them, ready at least in dress for the interview with Garman's mother. From the feeling in her toes, it would be days before she'd be able to wear pumps again.

The hallway was empty as she came out of the bedroom, no sign of either of the children. A small sign dangled from the knob of the bathroom door; it read VACANT. She smiled, turning it over to OCCUPIED, even though there seemed little danger of interruption.

She opened the door and a wave of heat hit her

in the face. The room was muggy from the water heater; windowless, there was no way for the heat to escape. There was a lock on the inside of the door, but, after examining it, she understood the need for the sign: the catch was flimsy enough to separate with a strong tug.

Three narrow steps led down into the bathroom, which was also long and narrow. Apparently there was no such thing as a common level to the rooms, even those on a common hallway. Another of Gabriel Gibson's tricks?

The gas lamp hissed surprisingly loudly on the marble-topped commode, casting a glare brighter than the small fixtures flanking the lavatory mirror could have produced. Marla hesitated at the top of the steps, nose wrinkling as she took in the decorations. Like the bedroom, the walls were half wainscoting, half papered, the design a hideous pattern of mermaids and Neptunes and seahorses in apparent chase of impossible fish.

The exposed woodwork was painted a matching sea-green, and the floor was covered with tiny octagonal green and white tiles. The equipment was obviously as old as the house and had never been updated, except for the addition of the wiring and the water heater. A partition hid that from those using the furnishings, although it was visible to anyone entering.

Marla closed the door, secured the lock, and walked down to the pedestaled toilet. A spider's web of tiny brown lines cracked it beneath the surface glaze. The tub was a monster, as high as her waist and sheathed in painted wainscoting. A movable step made it possible for the non-athletic to climb in and out. Tub and lavatory

61

fixtures were golden dolphins, the faucet handles ship's wheels. Rubber stoppers at the end of corroded brass chains seemed out-of-place beneath the gold equipment.

An open wall rack held thick towels and there was fresh soap in the dishes. Marla took a towel and a washcloth, the water gushing in the sink and splattering her robe until she reduced the pressure. The soap was richly scented, the perfume tickling her nose as she worked it into a lather and massaged it over her face. Her eyes closed while her fingertips rotated over and over. . . .

You're dawdling, girl. She eyed herself in the oval mirror, shocked by the redness of her eyes, highlighted by the white glare of the lower lamp. Get with it, Marla. You have to meet the dowager queen before you can collapse, so get it over with. When you come back, you can fall into that gorgeous bed.

Why did Tim have to spoil things by hinting at Alicia's temperament?

Sighing, Marla rinsed the soap from her face with the cloth, and brushed her teeth, and hurried through the rest of the quick freshening. It did help wake her a little, but she had to use her fingers to stretch her eyelids wide. As she toweled her face and neck, she eyed the tub wistfully, wondering what would happen if she ignored Alicia's summons altogether. A bath, and then bed . . .

No. Stop it! Get dressed, Marla; behave yourself!

Instinct made her spread the towel on a rack and turn the sign back to Vacant before she returned to the bedroom, moving quickly as she changed into the fresh clothing. Then she sat before the vanity mirror and loosened her hair, deciding she could spare two minutes for a brushing. The result was a definite improvement. Squinting, she could ignore the bags under her eyes. She looked younger, especially without makeup.

Makeup . . . Should she? She studied her face again, wondering if she looked too young. Common sense told her it would be foolish to use heavy cosmetics, but perhaps a bit of lipstick? Would Alicia approve?

Garman's mother must be at least in her sixties. In Alicia's day, good girls didn't use makeup. Play it safe, she decided: do without. Color could always be added later, if it didn't seem out-of-place, but better safe than sorry for the initial interview.

Her eyes closed of their own volition before Marla could push herself back from the vanity, and it was an effort to force them open. The temporary relief of washing was gone, the aftereffect only reinforcing her exhaustion. She shook her head, trying to stay alert, telling herself the interview was too important. She *must* make a good impression on Alicia Gibson.

Would Garman's mother like her? Would Bethel? Perhaps it had been a mistake to take a me-adult you-child stance with Corliss. The friendship of the children would be essential if the Gibson women were to be satisfied.

The room was suddenly shadowed as the sun passed behind a cloud. The curtains stirred again, then whipped violently into the room, the sharp breeze blowing Marla's hair across her cheek.

Shocked, she turned, to see the curtains still trembling, and swallowed as a cold sensation touched her spine.

Someone was watching her.

The corner of her eye caught movement in the mirror, and she turned far enough to see her own hands, pale as they rose against her body. The chill ran down her spine again, and she blinked, turning again to peer into the shadowy corners.

"Who's there?"

Someone *was* watching. . . .

Someone who hated her.

Marla swallowed. "I know you're there!"

Nothing. But the feeling remained. Fighting hysteria, Marla moistened dry lips as fear squeezed her chest. Her heart pounded impossibly loud, the sound seeming to come from outside her body. From someplace far away. The air was hard to breathe, heavy and cold.

"Skelly? Is that y-you?"

Her hand started to rise again, forefinger and thumb not quite touching; the fingers trembled, each digit by itself. She swallowed, and then again, trying to command her heart to slow its pounding as her eyes darted about.

"You may as well show yourself. I know you're there!" (Don't scream! He wants you to scream!) "Come out!"

Nothing. Nothing at all.

Seconds dragged, Marla listened; then she heard a measured tapping and jerked around suddenly. "What's that? What are you doing?"

Silence, but for the tapping. Biting her lip, and conscious of a sudden tension ache in her neck, she rose from the bench, her eyes falling on the table. Her watch was there; she picked it up, and the tapping resolved itself into the ticking of the mechanism. No other sound in the world, except for her own terrified breathing.

Her watch. Ticking. Marla uttered a single laugh, then swallowed the reflex, afraid of what would happen if she let herself go.

She felt eyes moving across her spine, sending the chill into each separate vertebra. He was behind her. She spun suddenly, knowing she could catch him.

The movement made her dizzy. But there was nothing, no one; except for herself, the room was empty.

Yet the watcher was there ... somewhere.

"Where are you?"

He's hiding, yes, that's it. Secret panels, secret rooms. . . . Tim hadn't been kidding! He's behind a secret panel, watching me with dirty eyes!

Madness. Marla closed her eyes, fingernails digging into her palms, until she could regain a measure of control. She blinked, and turned again, slowly.

"I know it's you, Skelly." She spoke slowly, enunciating each word with care. "This isn't funny. You've no right to spy on me. I want you to come out now!"

The room was empty. Her skin was clammy, but her neck burned with the embarrassment of being victimized by the voyeur—he was dirty, perverted, even if he was only a boy.

"I ... know it's you, Skelly."

It must be Skelly. Marla knew instinctively that the dirty eyes belonged to a child, a boy. He was insane—his father should have warned her.

Only a mad person could do this nasty business!
"Come out!"

She pressed her knuckles to her teeth and spun
around again. There were paintings on three of
the walls, inoffensive things that had barely captured her eye, unobtrusively colorless against the
wallpaper—the sort of pictures turned out by as-
sembly lines for cheap hotels. The frames were
plaster of paris, one chipped in several places and
showing white beneath the gilt.

He could be hiding behind one of the pictures.

Marla turned on each, staring until the moisture evaporated from her eyes and they burned.
By the door was a picture of a Dutch milkmaid,
the figure a gray-brown smear in the temporary
gloom.

The weight of the unseen malevolence was
heavy against her spine as Marla turned away
from the milkmaid; that picture was on the wall
common with the hall. He couldn't be there. Some
terrible burden of guilt was driving her down,
crushing her. . . .

"I've done nothing! Why are you doing this to
me? Leave me alone!"

You don't belong here

"What?"

Leave

Marla shuddered. The demand was strong in
her mind, chilling in its implications.

You must leave

"No!"

You will leave

"Stop! Stop . . ."

Where was he? *Where was he?* On the thin edge

66

of hysteria, Marla spun around, searching the shadowed corners of the room. Nothing.

Leave

The clown! The eyes are there, staring, watching, turning with her, following . . . he was in the next room. What was the color scheme? asked a detached portion of her mind, irrelevantly. Red? Yellow? *Which was it?*

Leave go away get out of here

"Don't! Please, don't do this to me. . . ."

A sob caught in Marla's throat, eyes stinging as she backed away, reached behind her to grab the bedpost, and spun around as though the movement would capture him, force him into the open. The eyes were on her, drilling into her from behind, no matter which way she turned. Come out! Come out, wherever you are . . . whoever you . . .

"Please!"

The sun broke free of the cloud cover, the room suddenly brightening, warmth touching Marla; then darkness again, massive shadows spreading along the walls. The sun lost its struggle with the clouds and the shadows thickened again, became pools of darkness spreading to touch the edge of the rug, spreading like spilled ink, spilled blood. . . .

She shuddered, closing her eyes, then forced them open again. Light—she needed light. In darkness lay madness, and she wouldn't share his insanity!

The clown was in the corner of her eye, drawing her around; the face was a colorless wash of blues, grays, and whites. Marla stared at it, swallowing again.

"I . . . I'll have to tell your father!"

Amusement ... sardonic? Why wouldn't he answer?

"I *know* it's you, Skelly!"

It had to be the boy; the malevolence was strongly male and very young, came from a child. Yet it was almost sexual in its intensity.

Leave. Must leave. Would leave ...

The wave of emotion that washed over her was stronger than before. She felt her knees weaken and staggered back until one hand banged against the bedpost; she sat down on the padded chest, the corner of the open suitcase scraping her thigh.

Leave leave leave

The outpouring of hatred was strong enough to crush her soul; single-minded, the command was a chant, pounding through Marla's brain, throbbing with each beat of her heart. Terrified, she could *feel* the demand through the soles of her feet, coming from the very fabric of the house.

Her heart pounded as she gasped, systole and diastole working her blood through her arteries, replenishing her body with vital oxygen but carrying the message of hatred into every shred of her being. The throbbing organ swelled in her chest until it felt too big to be contained.

Leave

"No! No, I can't...."

You willwillwill

"Please! Leave me alone!"

Never Leaveleaveleave

The guilt was intolerable, some ancient sin responsible. The pits of hell yawned until the stink of sulphur stung the membranes of her nostrils and she could feel the pain as fire licking her flesh. The stinging crossed the back of her hands, crawled up her arms. . . .

Leaveleaveleave

A rapping sounded, loud, and the chanting stopped as though chopped off by the executioner's blade. Marla gasped, fist against her mouth, and straightened, blinking as she looked around the room.

The rapping came again; it was no imaginary noise, did not come from her mind. She rose from the chest and took a hesitant step away from the bed.

Someone was knocking at the door.

"Come in!"

Her voice was a croak. The porcelain doorknob turned with maddening slowness. Time seemed to stop as Marla heard the click as the latch tongue came free of the receptacle.

The door opened.

Skelly stood there.

Five

The sun broke from blockade and warmth flooded into the bedroom. It touched the back of Marla's legs, rose over her, driving the chill before it. Cold sweat still coated her neck, but her back was warming and she felt her knees weaken in relief; moving back, she brushed the back of her hand across her mouth.

"Skelly!"

Relief came with the warmth. The invisible eyes were gone, vanished with the reappearance of the sun. The watcher couldn't have been Skelly. A smile contorted her mouth, the emotional storm no longer beating against her. No one hated her.

"Grandmother is waiting. Father sent me to ask you to hurry."

His eyes were unblinking, his voice solemn. The tremble was gone from Marla's fingers. She nearly laughed.

"Yes! I'll be right there."

The boy waited patiently, hand resting on the doorknob, while she cast another look about the bedroom—once more, nothing more than a comfortable chamber, a pleasant place in the summer warmth, made more comfortable by the breeze coming through the windows.

But the memory of terror was too strong to forget.

No. Marla bit her lip. She had imagined the whole episode; she was overwrought from exhaustion and the strain of recent weeks. No one was hiding in some secret place beyond the walls, no one was spying on her. Nothing but her imagination ...

Her glance touched the pictures, the milkmaid smiling as she swung her burden of pails from the yoke across her strong young shoulders. Across the room, the clown was only a clown, eternally clown-sad but carrying the secret ability to bring laughter. Opposite him, in a long narrow frame over the wing chair and centered between the left closet door and the outside wall, bright poppies bloomed, the strongest color in the room.

The closets ...

Forgetting Skelly's presence, Marla stared at the twin doors. If someone *had* been watching, wouldn't that be the most likely place?

The cold sweat had dried on her neck as she moved to the first closet, heart beating strongly again, caught the knob, and threw open the door. Dust motes swirled in the sudden rush of dead air, tickling her nose and almost making her sneeze.

Nothing.

The space was empty.

The closet was perhaps three feet deep, five wide, the walls entirely wainscoted; walls and floor were painted the same blue-gray as the room. A single high shelf held a broken hatbox, and a mixture of wooden and wire hangers hung from the thick wooden rod below. Half a dozen brass hooks were screwed into a narrow board beneath the shelf, the bases daubed, the painter too lazy to unscrew them before doing his work. It was the first mark of imperfection she had seen.

Marla stared into the closet for perhaps ten seconds, then closed the door and moved to the other. It proved a duplicate of the first, complete with dust and hangers, although its shelf was empty; the shelf was lined with much-folded, yellowed newspapers thumbtacked to the edge.

She backed away, her fingers giving enough push to swing the door closed. The memory of terror was still there, but fading; now it seemed no more than a bad dream.

Unconscious of the boy's presence, she glanced toward the porch, then swept the curtains aside to step through the French window. The sun was high although still below the zenith; its heat baked into her, contracting the sweat residue until her forehead seemed drawn. The sky was bright blue, fading into paleness near the horizon.

There were no clouds.

She couldn't have imagined it all . . . certainly not the shadows! The room *had* darkened. . . .

A tiny shiver touched a single low vertebra as Marla pressed her face to the screen, trying to see some of the roof overhead. There *must* be clouds. She couldn't be so close to the breaking point—

"Grandmother doesn't like to be kept waiting."

Skelly's voice brought her around, blinking. Marla nodded, came back into the room, and pushed past him into the hall. He closed the door and slipped past her.

One quick glance fell on the bathroom, but the boy's presence decided Marla against another stop, no matter how nice a wet washcloth would feel against her face. She frowned, sun-dried perspiration breaking into a thousand small scales that were invisible when her hand brushed her forehead.

The boy's bare feet glided silently over the carpeting. Marla could hear her own footsteps; they seemed almost as loud as her breathing. But Skelly seemed to float above the floor, unconnected to the real world. Ethereal, he moved through the corridor like a ghost. . . .

Stop it!

Stop . . . it.

Marla paused, clenching her fists; she was dangerously close to losing control again. There are no ghosts, no unseen watchers! There is nothing!

She drew back her shoulders and tossed her head. One more minute of this and she'd be screaming. Control—she must regain control before facing Garman and his mother.

Skelly turned the corner and Marla hurried after him, trying to force away the memory of terror. Nothing had happened except her overwrought imagination going wild. Think about other things—remember which way you're heading: north. If you don't remember the compass directions you could get lost. (No, not inside the walls! No!)

Head down, she hurried along the hallway, trying to catch up to Skelly. The stiff-starched gauze curtains over the windows were as proper as any in a prim Lyons Falls housewife's parlor, but the windows themselves were as varied as a jigsaw puzzle, as though the builder had tried to include one of every design. That one, now, was double-hung, and then she passed a tall, narrow casement, its turning crank covered by a curtain. After that came a multipaned antique that couldn't be opened at all.

They were past the corridor that led back to the main part of the house; several paces later, Marla looked to the left and saw a stairway climbing steeply to what must be the attics, although the stairs turned before reaching the top.

In that brief instant Skelly disappeared.

Marla stopped, panic returning. "Skelly!"

His head popped suddenly from the wall—another corridor, of course, located midway between two windows that were more widely spaced than the others. It was the only way he could have gone. Marla giggled nervously. It *was* the only way he could have gone.

Skelly withdrew, and Marla found him waiting two steps down, in a shadowed corridor far narrower and lower than any she had thus far seen. The ceiling pressed down scant inches over her head. The corridor might have been designed for children; a normal-size man would be forced to stoop. The walls were blank, with not even a light fixture breaking the gloomy pattern of the wallpaper.

"Isn't there a light?"

"There's a lamp ahead." He spoke softly, his voice pitched low for a child, as he led the way.

Thirty feet into increasing gloom, and then up four steps, the new extension suddenly widening to normal proportions, the ceiling retreating overhead. This stretch was as long as the first, and the walls were still blank. The end of the hall seemed completely filled by a massive mirror, but Marla was unable to make out more than the shifting of faint images. Locked away from the sun, her nervousness increased again.

A match scratched, orange flame touching the wick of a hurricane lamp. Now she saw a tiny pedestal table at the far end of the corridor, the only piece of furniture in the stretch; the top was barely wide enough to hold the lamp and the match holder. Skelly replaced the chimney and picked up the lamp.

"This way."

Another stairway cut through the right-hand wall at the very end of the hall, its wall blending with the frame of the mirror. Marla wondered how the massive thing could have been moved to its spot. Had the house been built around it? Perhaps the glass had come in first, the frame constructed in place.

She hurried after Skelly, each three steps of the stairs turning sharply to the right. The constant turns were dizzying, but the boy was skipping quickly ahead, sure of his footing. There was no handrail, although one would have been comforting.

Marla nearly walked into Skelly, who was waiting at the bottom, his hand on a doorknob. She gasped and started to apologize. He stared over the lamp, his eyes unblinking, until she flushed with embarrassment.

Then he opened the door and stepped into daylight.

Marla came out onto a second-level gallery much like the one above the main entrance, although here the staircase and the curving balustrade were of a dark, almost-black wood. The stairs swept down in the same grand manner, with a statue at bottom and one at the top.

But there were no smaller stairs leading up, and the skylight overhead was clear; it seemed farther away and perhaps was smaller. Across from her, not quite centered in the front wall, was a triangular window, point down. Higher placed than the bull's-eye, it showed only the sky. Cloudless sky.

Marla glanced over the railing and decided that they were several feet lower than the gallery above the main entrance—either that, or the first level below was higher. But she could see a single door leading out to the screened section of the porch, and the back of a swing was visible through a flanking window.

She had imagined the watcher. . . .

Garman came out of a room across the gallery, the only other door opening onto this level. The walls here were blank except for a single massive oil portrait directly opposite the door across the well. It showed a middle-aged man in starched collar and four-buttoned suit; he resembled Garman. His father?

"Ah, Miss Doren! Mother is waiting."

He came to meet her halfway, and led her to the door, which was heavy with carving and stained the same dark color as the staircase.

"Are you feeling better?" His voice was throaty again, filled with reassuring heartiness.

"Yes, thank you," lied Marla. "To be honest, these last few days have been hectic, and I didn't sleep last night."

"After you meet Mother we'll let you go, I promise. The children can survive another day on their own. Lunch is at one, but if you wish, Mrs. Davis can send a tray to your room."

"I don't think I could eat."

Marla became aware of empty space; turning, she saw no one. Skelly had disappeared again.

She shivered. She hadn't heard him depart, but the door to the staircase was closed again. The lamp was on another small table, extinguished. She was sure that the table had been empty.

The boy's ability to move so quietly disturbed her, heightened her nervousness. Could he in some way have been responsible for the incident in the bedroom?

No; forget it! It never happened. Pay attention to what you're doing now. Forget that silly episode. You imagined it all.

She took a deep breath, steeling herself for the coming confrontation, as Garman opened the door and held it for her.

Marla entered the tower. And stopped. Garman was crowding on her heels.

For the second time today she felt as though she'd wandered onto a movie set—a black-and-white movie, this time. The room before her was immense, walls curving around in a perfect circle, half glass and half bare painted plaster. A decorator had been at work here, too, but it couldn't possibly have been the man who did her bedroom.

Marla blinked repeatedly as her eyes tried to adjust to the brighter light; it reflected off surfaces either stark white or pitch black, scarcely muted by the latter. The black, polished and unpolished, emphasized the glare rather than complementing it.

The room was a designer's fantasy of Park Avenue ultramodern. Marla's eyes swept it, drawn first to the glass wall and then caught by the spiral staircase that cut through the center of the ceiling, twelve feet above. It was so much like a movie set that she almost expected to see Rosalind Russell come swinging down, skirts swirling.

. The silliness of the thought lightened her mood, helped push the earlier disturbing thoughts down where they belonged. Later she could work at burying them completely.

There were two levels to the tower; the drapes, pulled back from the glass wall, disappeared through the ceiling. She wondered what supported the disc of the floor above; the staircase wasn't enough.

The staircase was wrought iron, carpeted in an alternate pattern of black and white that blended at the base with the zebra-striped room carpeting. The latter stretched from wall to wall, seamless. The room was at least forty feet across, and the massive pieces of furniture were properly proportioned.

Her eyes passed over twin Chinese ebony cabinets standing on either side of a white brick fireplace, the latter almost small in comparison with the general scale. Over the fireplace, stretching out above either cabinet, was an abstract painting at least ten feet wide. Marla was unfamiliar with Jackson Pollock, and in the brief instant that her eyes touched the painting, she decided that she didn't like it; but it provided the only touch of color to the scheme.

Near the door was a glass-fronted ebony bookcase, the lowest half holding about a dozen leatherbound books. The shelves above carried an array of silver-framed photographs. In the second that she spared to glance at the collection, she spotted the man in the oil portrait and at least two of the boys in the photos above the main entrance.

The constant swirl of black and white made Marla's head spin; she made the mistake of trying to follow the pattern of the carpet, and blinked, her eyes jumping about, hurting when they rested too long on one object. She glanced toward the glass wall again and spotted a breakfast set, wrought iron with polished ebony top. It was circled by four chairs, also wrought iron, which would have seemed better suited as patio furniture.

Perpendicular to the fireplace was a white couch, fourteen feet long; low-backed, it was piled with white cushions. In a less bizarre setting the couch would have been the most impressive piece of all. The woman sitting there was almost lost in her surroundings.

Alicia Gibson perched in the mathematical center of the couch, a silver tea set on the ebony coffee table before her, near her right hand. The tea set was antique, ornate, and seemed out-of-place in the starkly modern room.

"Well? Don't just stand there!"

Alicia's voice was brittle with age but whip-sharp. Marla advanced into the room, Garman following to close the door. As she heard it settle into its frame, she felt as though she were locked away from the outside world, and knew rising panic again. What was she doing here?

"Ah, my dear Mrs. Gibson!" she said.

A man jumped from a black wing chair facing Alicia. A matching white chair completed the conversation group, although there were two other, more intimate arrangements, on the near and far sides of the room. The man spoke exuberantly, a delicate bone-china cup almost lost in his long, supple fingers. How had she overlooked him? He seemed impossibly tall, towering over the woman on the couch. A little black waxed mustache twitched as he clicked his heels together.

"This must be, this is, the new governess. How charming! Welcome, my dear, to Beechhaven!"

He wore formal morning clothes, his voice carrying the trace of an accent. He beamed approval, bent eight degrees from the vertical, chin cocked away as pleasure radiated from every pore.

Marla fought the impulse to laugh; the breaking of tension was the relief she needed. He stood several inches over six feet, and was the very caricature of a movie Frenchman—handsome, if you could forget the pomaded hair and the ridiculous mustache. His brown eyes sparkled. He seemed too oily to be anything but the villain called for by the scriptwriter who had designed this setting. Dressed as he was, he could have come from a wedding. Or a wedding cake.

"Sit down, Philippe! You know you make me

nervous when you jump about so," Alicia said crossly.

His heels clicked again, his bottom touching the edge of the chair as his fingers deposited his cup on the table and in the same smooth motion flicked his tails out of the way.

"A thousand pardons, madame."

Then he was on his feet again as Garman brought Marla across the room and made the formal introductions. Alicia acknowledged her with a single brisk nod.

"This is Philippe Crateau," added Garman, almost as an afterthought.

The mysterious Philippe—the other guest. Marla remembered he was North, and wondered what was the color scheme of his room. Crateau was several years younger than Garman, although his formal costume and pomaded hair made it difficult to guess his exact age. He bowed again, reaching for Marla's fingers, and for a nervous moment she thought he was going to kiss her hand. She felt relief when he did no more than hold her fingertips briefly.

"My great pleasure, m'mselle—Marla, is it not?"

She nodded. "Thank you, Monsieur."

"No, no! No formalities here, are there, Madame?" He glanced around at Alicia. "You must call me Philippe. Here everything, everyone, is democratic, which perhaps is the one good thing to come of this terrible war."

Alicia cut him off. "Go along, Philippe. We'll continue our discussion another time."

"But of course." Heels clicked again. "Until your convenience, Madame. M'mselle. Garman."

A bow, a brisk dip of his head to Garman, and he was gone. Marla saw the twisted smile on Garman's face as he watched Philippe disappear. He reminded her of the clown, but smiling. The thought of ghosts, of unseen watchers, was suddenly ridiculous. She *had* imagined the whole thing. . . .

"Look at me!"

Alicia's voice cracked again and Marla's head snapped around. She knew embarrassment, felt like an errant schoolgirl.

"That's better." Alicia nodded, sitting erect; she leaned forward to deposit her cup on the table, then folded her hands in her lap. She was taller than Marla had first thought, the disparity created by the contrast with Philippe. She wore a severely tailored gray suit that at first seemed as out-of-place in this mountain setting as the decor of this improbable room.

Woman and room were a match, however. The feeling of fantasy was still strong for Marla; perhaps she was dreaming all this, and would wake up in her bed at home to find that the world had gone back to normal. (But when was normal? What year did she want it to be . . . 1938? . . . 1937?)

The family resemblance between mother and son, grandmother and grandchildren, was unmistakable. The jaw was firm and strong in all the generations. Corliss and Skelly had inherited good genes and would grow up as attractive as their forebears. Not beautiful: Alicia was as handsome as Garman, discounting the age difference.

She reminded Marla of someone else, however, and after a moment's puzzlement it came to her:

Andy Hardy's aunt, in the movies. Alicia had the same uncompromising expression, the same aquiline nose, her eyes as bright and as intensely blue as the children's. Pince-nez dangled from a ribbon, but she needed no glasses as she examined Marla.

Marla's eyes wandered; she felt uncomfortable before the direct gaze of the older woman. She forced herself to look back, blinking rapidly. Alicia's silver-blue hair was carefully marcelled, and Marla wondered who did it for her. There had been no mention of a hairdresser. If someone came in, she would have to take advantage of the service.

Wake up, Marla! Your mind is wandering.

Every curl of Alicia's was in place. Garman's mother wore no makeup, and Marla was glad she had decided against any for herself. A coral cameo brooch was at her throat, and a small gold watch was pinned by a short chain to her breast. She wore no wedding band, but a large diamond solitaire glittered almost vulgarly on the ring finger of her left hand.

"Sit down! I dislike looking up at people."

Marla sat quickly, peevishly obeying the order, in the chair abandoned by Philippe; the cushion still bore the imprint of his bony shape. The plush upholstery seemed hot against the backs of her legs.

"Tea?"

"Thank you, yes." She didn't even like tea.

"Lemon or cream?"

"Neither, thank you. One lump of sugar."

Alicia completed the ritual of pouring and Marla accepted her part of the social burden, the cup rattling until she lowered it to her lap. Duty completed, Alicia returned her hands to her lap, carefully manicured fingers composed. Marla stirred vigorously, short, nervous strokes, then realized that she was banging the spoon against the cup.

She placed the spoon on the saucer and carefully brought the cup to her lips. Nearly a minute had passed, Garman keeping to the background and beyond Marla's line of sight, before Alicia spoke again, as though confirming a statement made by one of the others.

"It has been unusually warm, but at least the black flies have not been as annoying as usual."

Had Marla missed something? She blinked, the cup still at her lips, untasted. The lump of sugar was only half dissolved, despite her nervous stirring. She sipped; the tea was bitter, the tannic acid coating her tongue and the inside of her lips, but she decided against stirring again.

"At four each afternoon the children join me for tea. I do not permit them to be tardy."

She *had* missed something. Alicia stood, ramrod straight, as tough as the wrought iron that supported so much of her surroundings. She was of another generation, yet she belonged here; the room bore the stamp of her personality. Alicia too was stark, her personality monotoned.

Garman's mother moved toward the stairs, then paused with one hand on the iron railing; Marla knew she was waiting for her to leave.

More and more curious, she felt as though she had dropped down the rabbit hole. Was Alicia the Queen of Hearts? (Not Alice! Most certainly not.)

Marla glanced around and saw Garman waiting by the door, his hands on the knob. At this moment he looked very like his son, perhaps because they held themselves the same way. That must be in the genes too.

Marla moved toward him but didn't turn until he closed the door behind her. During the brief interview Alicia had never so much as said goodday, nor used her name.

"Do you need a guide?"

"Pardon?" Garman spoke pleasantly, but Marla was still distracted by the strange interview with his mother. "I'm sorry; what did you say?"

"To find the way back to your room," he amplified. "Guests find it difficult at first."

"Oh." She saw the door on the other side of the gallery. "No. No, thank you. I remember the way from here."

"Tomorrow morning the children can give you the grand tour. Things really aren't as confusing as they seem—there is method to the madness. You'll learn. In a week you'll be an old hand."

He was prattling, like Corliss, running on about nothing at all. For the first time Marla realized that Garman was hiding nervousness himself, and now she was sure that she had missed something during the interview.

Did she still have the job? Of course; he had said nothing to indicate otherwise. The meeting with Alicia had accomplished nothing, unless it was to give Alicia a close look at her. (Designed to give *her* a look at the mistress of Beechhaven?)

She almost permitted the flow of questions to

start, then changed her mind. Despite Garman's surface affability, enough tension had showed to tell her that the note was false. He was transparently afraid of his mother, whether or not he was an internationally important business-man.

Questions could wait until she collared Tim and could demand a complete fill-in on the strange in-habitants of Beechhaven. Marla knew she was competent; she could do the job Garman had hired her to do—tutor and guard and den mother Corliss and Skelly in any way necessary, or in any way demanded by their grandmother.

"Will you want lunch?"

Marla was surprised to find that she was hun-gry; she answered in the affirmative as they crossed the gallery, then Garman went down-stairs. She turned to the stair door, hand on the knob before she remembered the lamp; she reached to take it from the table.

Matches. She had to light the lamp.

There was none, although she had noticed hold-ers and dishes of matches scattered about the house. She'd have to start carrying a packet. She opened the door, nervous again at the thought of darkness above the first turn. Go downstairs, take the porch to the main entrance, and trace the path to her room from there?

The idea was silly. It would take no more than a minute to go up these stairs and through the dark halls to daylight again. Less, if she hurried.

Leaving the door open, she started up; two turn-ings, and she could no longer see her own pale flesh. Marla drew quick breaths, heart beating faster, nostrils catching the smell of old wood and with it the dust of at least sixty years. Not the dust of the closets: that was heavier, oily from a paint job hastily slapped on, too thick in the cracks of the wainscoting, and still moist beneath the surface even after a year or more.

Counting risers, she was up fifteen steps. Primal fear of darkness made her heart pound loudly, until she heard the voices from above.

Marla stopped, looked up; they were directly overhead, although some distance above. What was up there? It must be the attic.

She touched the wall, feeling a resurgence of panic at the close surroundings. Then the voices came more strongly, the first an indistinguishable mumble, followed by the clear words of a girl: Corliss.

"I don't care! I like her, no matter what Skelly says. You can't hurt her—I won't let you!"

Six

Marla froze, breath held. . . .

(She doesn't mean you. They're not talking about you.)

Her throat suddenly dry, the closeness of the staircase constricting her lungs, she strained to hear what they were saying. A corner of her mind told her that she was eavesdropping, and eavesdroppers hear things they don't want to hear, but she shunted the thought aside. Her eyes burned dry again, and she blinked.

Mumble . . . A boy. Skelly? No, it couldn't be; Corliss's words had made it clear that she was talking to someone else.

Marla went up another step, hand sliding along the wall until suddenly her fingers curled around the corner; she had lost track of the risers. Her momentum carried her beyond the corner; her elbow cracked sharply, and the pain brought red sparks to her eyes.

She pulled back, turning, and smacked her hip into the wall. The cry caught in her throat before it could escape—they would hear. They mustn't hear her.

Listen; what are they doing up there? Corliss,

who are you talking to? (To whom are you talking? corrected the tutorial censor in her mind.)

Silence. Marla had almost decided that they had gone when the mumbler spoke again, his voice lower this time, almost drowned out by the sound of her own breath and the rush of her blood. Although the words couldn't be deciphered, she was sure the speaker was a boy.

"No, Andrew!" Corliss again, almost crying in her agitation. Thank you for identifying him, Corliss—but who is Andrew? "You can't!'

A word of counterpoint followed, almost forceful enough for Marla to understand. The argument grew more heated. Shamed by her attitude, Marla held breath again, trying to make out what he was saying.

Corliss: "If you do, I—I'll never come back!"

Silence again, while the unseen Andrew considered the threat. Corliss was clearly upset, but Marla couldn't be sure of Andrew's emotions. Then the mumble came again, more forceful . . . derisive.

"No, he won't!" Corliss, triumphant. "I won't let Skelly come either—you know he does whatever I say. We'll both stay away, and you'll be all alone again."

Marla waited for the reply, sweat beading on her forehead. Say something, Andrew! Say something . . .

Nothing. She started up another step, fingertips probing ahead to touch the rounded edge of the riser. Where were they? Is that a crack, light? No; it was just a false streak across her vision.

The children must be close, only a few feet

above her. The stairwell acted as a conduit for their voices. If only she could hear Andrew's words more clearly.

A single dragging sound, dull and moving away. Marla held her breath again, this time for nearly twenty seconds, but nothing more happened. The participants had left the field of battle.

Now what was that all about?

(Not you, Marla. Not you.)

Who was Andrew? She hadn't heard that there was another boy at Beechhaven—perhaps he was the son of one of the servants. The Davises? (Dour Davis, a father? Improbable.) The stable master, Cassini?

Whatever his parentage, he sounded like a vicious little sort. Marla formed an image: pointed chin, tight pinched nose, eyes too close together. A street rat from Dickens; or the spoiled son of an Alger rich man, out to do dirt to the plucky hero. When he was good he was very, very good, but when he was bad he was horrid. (Except he's never good.) Speak to Garman? Perhaps Corliss and Skelly should be warned to avoid the boy.

(He couldn't mean to hurt you, Marla. No matter how vicious a brat, he has no reason to hurt you.)

The thought was dangerous, so she pushed it away, censor burying it deep in the tight box kept in the darkest bottom corner of her mind. Light was never permitted to enter there, the top of the box never cracked. The things inside couldn't be allowed to escape. Keep the mind box closed and you'll never have to admit that the nightmares of childhood still live, still come out when your guard is down, when you're tired, sick, frightened, despairing. . . .

Trembling, nearly soaked with perspiration, Marla straightened, her fingers trailing the wall. (My, but it's warm here.) The implications of Corliss's words had frightened her, and she couldn't deny her state of mind. But why? She had done nothing wrong, there was nothing dangerous in her own thoughts; there was no reason for her heart to be pounding.

(Sadworrysickhurtpain) No! No . . .

Take a breath, deep, that's it. Everyone had sad things they want to forget, the unhappy times in life when loved ones die or get sick, troubled moments when nothing seems to go right, even the betrayal of lovers (Tim). Everyone has regrets, moments when the past comes back to haunt them.

"You're being foolish!"

She spoke aloud, her own scolding words startling her. She was being silly—no one wanted to hurt her. (There are no unseen watchers hiding in the walls.) She was tired and needed sleep.

Her head throbbed; yes, sleep. A good night's rest and the world would return to normal. Beechhaven is a haven, and you will spend the next two months recovering from the strains of the last two years. It is nothing more. (Foolish house, yes; built by a practical joker with more money than sense.)

It is not a place of ghosts and perverted minds! It isn't . . .

(Don't go, Mama—lock the window. Stay with me, don't let the bad things in. Stay!)

91

Marla dropped her hands to her sides, eyes closed—no; open them. Look up, watch the stairs. Hold your hands against your legs until the trembling stops. It will stop. You have a headache, but soon you can rest, sleep.

She reached one hand to the wall and started up the stairs. It wasn't far, just another turn or two and she'd be in the hallway. Her legs resumed the mechanical motions of climbing, moving her through the darkness as she emptied her mind of every thought but that of bath and bed.

Two more turns did bring her to the gloomy corridor, the great mirror suddenly sliding down as she rose to its level. For an instant, panic froze her again, then she managed a small laugh. Her imagination was running away.

(Why am I running? Stop me! Stop me!)

She stumbled on the steps and fell into the smaller corridor, hands out to fend off the close walls. Breath slammed from her lungs as she careened from wall to wall, then stumbled again, banging her knee on the last step.

Daylight. Her hands slammed against the rear wall of the house, the shock sending stinging pain through her heels and her arms. She was all right, all right. . . .

Marla blinked repeatedly as her eyes readjusted to the daylight coming through the lace curtains. Brushing her hand across her mouth, she pushed away from the wall. Her heart was slowing its mad pace. Her breath hissed over her teeth, loud in her ears, and she wiped her mouth again and licked the sour taste from its roof.

Breath deep; hold it; relax.

Three more deep breaths followed, the sour stick of her sweat, strengthened by fear, filling her nose. Breathe in, precision, breathe out: see, the trembling has stopped. (Almost) Laugh, Marla, at how silly you've been acting. Ha. Ha ha.

A giggle burst from her lips and then was swallowed back. Marla knew she was being foolish; there was nothing to fear in darkness. (The ark of the dark, the terrible dark ship rushing you away to the river Styx, to the punishment place, to the burning place)

Stop! Stop . . . it. You stopped asking for a nightlight when you were ten, remember? Certainly you remember. The year Mother died. (Mama)

A bath, yes. Get out of these clothes and into hot water—even the fresh blouse was dirty now, soiled by her sweat, and the need to wear it over a body unwashed and dirty from the train ride and the heat.

(Hold out your hand, Marla, fingers wide. See? They aren't trembling.)

Marla began to move, thinking of bath and promised lunch—God, she was famished! How long since breakfast? It seemed like days. Her stomach rumbled, a reminder of emptiness stronger even than physical exhauston. Eat first, then to bed.

(There's a name for people who think others are trying to hurt them: paranoid)

Heartbeat almost normal, she glanced through the first window she passed and was reassured by the gardens below; the green forest seemed only an arm's reach away. The pine-shrouded mantle

93

of the Adirondacks stretched purple-gray against the horizon, the road to the railroad tracks an interrupted ribbon-gash where the land beyond the second knoll rose far enough to let her see it. No other clearings or houses broke the stretch of forest.

Marla started to pass the next window, then stopped, holding the curtain aside. Just below the level of the window was a sloping section perhaps ten feet wide and two or three times that long. What could it be?

She pictured the back of the house seen from ground level, vague but for the track of the circling porch; this must be the section rising to Gabriel Gibson's bedroom. Now that Marla had seen the view from the front of the house, it seemed even stranger Gabriel should have chosen this location for his private quarters.

(After Alicia's tower lair, what had the master of Beechhaven built for himself?)

The stretch of porch was short enough; the room couldn't be much larger than her own. Marla could see the roofs of the outbuildings through the trees at the bottom of the hill. Perhaps Gabriel only wanted to be away from his wife—no; she had refused to live here at all.

Another whim of the architect—Garman had said there was method to the madness, but as yet it eluded Marla. The house was built as though Gabriel had strived for confusion, piling section blocks haphazardly and akimbo. Hollow blocks, where the denizens lived. Apparently no two rooms were permitted to share the same floor level, continuity being an affront to Gabriel's eye.

Had he conducted his business affairs in that

manner? Unlikely; the fortune would never have survived. But Gabriel must have been a little mad—certainly no completely sane person could have built this house.

(Can the mad recognize others afflicted with madness?)

Marla moved on, feeling almost normal now. Her own room was just ahead. Go in the bathroom first, start the water in the tub. . . .

Sudden impulse stopped her before she could turn into the shorter corridor, the red-trimmed door within reach of her hand. She was tired, and this was no time to be exploring, but her hand reached out, caught the knob, and turned it.

She faced another door, eighteen inches beyond the first; the short walls and the ceiling between were totally mirrored, reflecting the deep red that was the sole color of the second door. Marla stared a few seconds, then images of her pale hand flashed around her as she reached for the doorknob.

The room was heavy with gloom, faint light coming through slits in closed shutters over the windows in the two outside walls. Marla blinked, and nearly backed out again; then her eyes adjusted. She was in a boudoir, not a bedroom; the chamber seemed lifted from the last century.

The hinges squeaked as she pushed the door in the last few inches, dim light flashes pulling her eyes up to a crystal chandelier. The facets of the dangling prisms reflected fragments of her image, aided by the light coming from the corridor.

The room was heavy with heat, the air close after being shut in a long time. The windows were framed by heavy, tassel-fringed velvet drapes that were caught partway by silken ropes. Marla saw a hurricane lamp and reached for a match in the holder beside it. She struck the match, removed the chimney, and passed the flame over the wick holder.

Nothing: no light. The flame almost burned her fingers before she realized that the wick was turned down too far. Feeling foolish, she blew out the match and rolled the burled knob until the scorched end of the cotton wick appeared above the slit in the brass. Another match brought the wick to life, the flame shooting high; she replaced the chimney, which promptly blackened along one side. The cloying stink of burning kerosene seemed sickening until she turned the wick down again.

(What are you doing here? The bath, Marla!)

Held in her hand, the lamp dispelled the near shadows, although it was too weak to reach more than a few feet away. Everything about her was massive, dark mahogany and red velvet plush. Marla turned, lifting the lamp high, and saw a portrait to her right: an oil, in a heavy oval frame. The subject was a young woman, tresses piled high in Gibson-girl fashion, her neck impossibly long, regally swelling bosom bare almost to the point of obscenity. A haughty smile touched the corners of the painted woman's mouth, her dark eyes flashing.

"I beg your pardon!"

Marla stepped back, aware that she had spoken the apology aloud. Who was the woman? Someone who had used this room? Perhaps Gabriel hadn't minded his wife's reluctance to stay at Beech-haven. . . .

No; she might just as easily be Gabriel's wife, Garman's grandmother. Embarrassed, Marla tried to blow out the lamp, then burned her fingers as she grabbed the chimney. At last she came to her senses and turned the wick down until the flame died, then replaced the lamp on the table and backed from the room, closing both doors. She had no right to be here.

(Wouldleave)

No; shut the thought away. It was only her imagination. Go across the hall, never mind the yellow room—you don't care what's there, it's none of your affair. Start the bath so it will be ready by the time you're undressed. It's getting late, lunch will be here soon, finish the bath first, then eat, then bed. . . .

The thought was forgotten; she entered the bathroom and hurried down the three steps to start the tub. Water gushed, steam rising in seconds as the hot water coming from the heater pushed out the cold water standing in the pipe. She tested the temperature with her fingers and found it almost scalding; she adjusted the level, then cut the force so that the tub wouldn't fill before she came back.

In the bedroom, Marla undressed and was belting her robe and shoving her toes into her slippers in less than a minute. She started to turn to the door, and the spill of cosmetics where she had dumped them on the vanity caught her eye. Amid the jumble was an octagonal bottle of bubble bath, a Christmas present last year from Charley Jefferson. Marla had priced it later in Emden's

Pharmacy at sixty-nine cents. At least it was nicer than the dime-store perfume Charley usually gave her.

She smiled as she picked up the bottle, thinking of Charley's well-meant intentions. She had packed it without thinking, throwing it in among the other items while hurrying to finish last night. She'd never used one of Charley's presents before ... but why not?

Marla turned the sign on the bathroom door and twisted the catch for insurance. The dolphin faucets were still spilling enthusiastically, and the tub was half filled. There must be a tank in the attic, perhaps cisterns to catch and store rainwater. Otherwise it would call for a powerful pump to raise water this high and with such force.

Marla caught up her hair and wrapped it securely in a towel, checking the ends of the turban in the mirror. The gas light showed clearly the smudges across her face—had she looked that way in the tower? No wonder Alicia had cut the interview short! She might not have washed her face at all, for all the good the earlier trip to the bathroom had done her.

A hag stared from the mirror, a face ancient with age, circles etched deep around the eyes. Marla shuddered; the only beauty cure for this was sleep.

The tub was ready. She poured in bubble bath, foam rising quickly above the rim, then took one of the bath towels from the rack, draping it over a wooden stool that she moved close to hand. The towel was the largest she had ever seen, and incredibly thick; the pile seemed as soft as velvet.

She crushed the fabric in her fingers, reluctant to release it. Beechhaven had its drawbacks, but even under conditions that must seem primitive to them, the Gibsons knew how to surround themselves with comfort.

Into the water: she mounted the step and swung her leg over the rim, one heel pushing through the foam to touch the water—and she yelped, drawing her foot back. Too hot!

But heat was needed, would release the tensions of sore muscles and tired flesh. Balancing on the step, she winced as she lowered the foot back into the water. The heat came over the calloused bottom of her heel and lapped at her ankle, until she could tolerate the temperature level. Then down, water rising above calf, knee, thigh, until the ball of the foot touched the bottom of the tub.

The other foot went under more easily, Marla standing a moment as steam rose to dampen her body. She flexed her fingers, then lowered herself gingerly, gasping at the first splash against her buttocks, then enjoying the deep penetration of the heat, which was already easing the aches.

She sat, for a moment breasts floating on the surface among the foam as she clung to the edge of the tub. Then she let her arms drop until they hit the water, and floated, fingers splayed out and bobbing as the water surged around her body. Then, knees bent, she began the final slide down into the water, water rising over her arms and coming up to her throat, stray bubbles popping against her face and tickling her nose until she brought one hand back to the surface and pushed them away.

Her eyes closed. Heaven!

Forgotten were the disquieting, frightening experiences of the day as Marla surrendered to the embrace of the bathwater. There were no problems important enough to worry her now, no eyes spying, no children making strange threats. She gave herself to the sybaritic pleasures of the bath, the noblest invention of man, burying the bad thoughts. The outside world vanished: the distant war, the circumstances responsible for her presence here, were stray annoyances, not worth consideration. She breathed in the cheap, piney scent of Charley Jefferson's bubble bath and under it the harsher tang of mineral-rich water.

(Who is Andrew?)

Stop thinking; pick up the sponge, bring it over your breasts, squeeze out the water, and open your mouth as your head falls back. Enjoy. Enjoy ...

Marla blinked and sat up straight. The turban towel was dripping onto her shoulders, and the water seemed tepid.

How long had she been asleep?

She brushed the back of her hand across her face where bubbles had dried on her nose and blew the residue from her upper lip. The bath water was cooler and the bubble bath had dissipated into tiny thin patches. There was no longer heat enough to let her relax, sink down, let the back of the tub support her head ...

But bed would be infinitely better. Marla shook her head and stood, releasing the dripping tur-

100

ban. The bottom of her hair was soaked. Should she leave the tub for another towel?

The necessary effort was too great. She lowered herself again, holding her head high, she began the mechanical functions of washing. At the same moment, her awareness of hunger increased; it must be nearly time for the promised lunch tray. If not, perhaps she could go down to the kitchen and beg at least milk before surrendering to bed.

Sluicing away the last of the suds, she stood, rising from the water like Venus at dawn, and sighed with pleasure. Tired muscles had relaxed; gone were the worrisome fears. The idea that someone had been spying on her, had threatened her, was laughable. She was tired, that was all.

Marla hooked the chain of the stopper with her big toe, the water rushing away into the depths of the house, the whirlpool gurgling noisily. She watched the water swirl as she toweled herself, wondering what contortions the plumbing followed before it exited the house. Visions of cobwebby depths, dank crawl spaces, and dripping cellars made her wrinkle her nose. She pushed the thoughts away. Don't think about bad things, and they can't happen.

She donned her robe, shaking out her wet hair, and stood before the mirror to comb it out. As she finished, the gas lamp suddenly flickered, then began to dim.

"Oh!" Marla turned, staring at the light; then she bent over it, peering at the mantles beneath the metal shade. A white coal seemed to glow amid yellowish light.

Unsure how to adjust it, she touched the little

wheel on the base, trying to turn it. It resisted, then turned freely, but the lamp only dimmed further.

Leave it for someone who knew what he was doing. She was finished here anyway. By the time Marla reached the door, the fire box of the water heater glowed almost as dimly as the lamp. Thank God she'd awakened when she had—otherwise she'd have finished her bath in the dark.

Marla returned to her bedroom, leaving the door ajar. There were many things she'd have to learn how to do this summer, adjusting to the lack of amenities she had taken for granted. There were farms around Lyons Falls that still did not have electricity, but she was thankful she'd been born at a time and in a place where twentieth century conveniences were available to all.

She finished checking her appearance in the vanity mirror, satisfied, and donned pajamas from her suitcase; she would wait until tomorrow to finish unpacking. She took the dresses to the closet, slipping them onto wood hangers, and was in the act of turning down the comforter when a diffident tap sounded at the door.

"Come in?" No need to be apprehensive!

The door opened a crack and a young girl peered around the edge . . . cringing. "Your lunch, miss."

"Oh!" Marla felt relief. "Come in!" She indicated a small table. "Put it there, please."

The girl sidled through the doorway, staying as far from Marla as the furniture allowed. She moved in short, quick steps, the tray clattering as she dropped her burden.

102

"I'm sorry, miss!"

Eyes darted as though expecting a blow. The girl, wearing an ill-fitting maid's uniform, seemed scarcely older than Corliss. Her hands grabbed for the tray to square it with the edge of the table, then moved it half an inch to the left.

"It's all right," Marla said kindly. "Thank you."

"Yes, miss."

The girl edged away, chewing on her lower lip, as Marla sat down at the table. As soon as the way was clear, she scooted for the door, then stopped as though struck when Marla asked:

"What's your name?"

"Callie, miss." Her throat trembled, reminding Marla of a frightened gray mouse she had once trapped in her kitchen. The girl's posture was bad, made worse by head bent submissively until her eyes were forced to roll up to see anyone above her.

"You don't have to be afraid, Callie." The edging toward freedom stopped, one hand sliding protectively over the other and both clutching her stomach. "Where are you from?"

"Boonville."

Marla smiled. "Then we're neighbors—I'm from Lyons Falls." The villages were only ten miles apart. "Have you worked here long, Callie?"

She shook her head. "Come Monday, miss."

Then she was one of the sisters who had replaced the departing Angie. Why was she so frightened? She remembered Tim's description of the treatment the girls received from Alicia and Bethel.

Or had Callie felt spying eyes and overheard conversations?

"Miz Davis wants me in the kitchen, miss. I got to go."

Marla sipped at the glass of milk and found it biting cold. "All right, Callie."

The girl fled, almost banging the door but turning to catch it at the last instant. Marla picked up her fork, but before she could touch the food a yawn split her face. She glanced at the food; her appetite had vanished. Another sip of milk, and then bed . . .

She covered the tray with the napkin and stretched as she stood, then unbelted the robe and let it fall to the chair. Her watch was on the marble-topped stand, close to the bed. She glanced at it, then dropped across the mattress, one foot kicking at the folded sheet. Before she could pull the sheet over her legs she was asleep. . . .

Marla opened her eyes suddenly, wide awake. Moonlight came through the French windows, the spill on her right cutting across the bottom corner of the bed, the other hitting the wall and the closet.

How long had she slept? She turned her head, reached for her watch, then twisted around to bring it into the moonlight. Eleven-seventeen. Ten hours, a little more.

The sound came again, the noise that had awakened her from sound sleep. Marla whipped around, nostrils flaring, heart speeding; her forehead was beaded with sweat, although the night air was almost cool.

Silence. She stared at the closet; the sound

had come from there, a faint dragging. Swallowing nervously, she rose to her feet. "Who is it?"

Nothing.

She reached for the nearest lamp, hands trembling as they struck the match. The orange flare seemed no brighter than the moonlight. Lamp before her, Marla advanced toward the closet, reached for the knob . . . hesitated. She drew a deep breath and threw the door open; it banged against the chest. Dust rushed out with the lowering of air pressure, and something struck her face. . . .

Seven

"Oh—*oh*!"

Marla took a step back, the reflex turning her
away, and the cry escaping as her hands came up
to ward off the thing clinging to her body. The
lamp nearly slipped from her grasp; she juggled
it, but the brass clips holding the chimney were
loose, and the glass fell and bounced on the carpet. Her free hand was batting away whatever
had struck her. It slid down her body, a white
shroud, and glided to the carpet. The hot glass
rolled against her bare foot.

"Ouch!"

More shocked than hurt, she jumped again,
backing into the bedpost and cracking her head
on it. Marla caught the post, seeing stars, and
held on for a moment while she gathered herself.
Then she sat on the edge of the mattress to rub
her injured foot.

A yellowed newspaper, open and tented above
the fold, lay on the carpet.

"Oh, my!"

Feeling foolish, Marla managed a small laugh.
Just a newspaper, slipped from the closet shelf.
She laughed again and pressed her hand to her

breast, as though the pressure would slow the pace of her heart.

Only a newspaper . . .

It's just your nerves, Marla! she told herself. Relax—take a deep breath. She sighed from her throat, breast rising and then falling deeply. Another. That's the way, calm down.

Normally she didn't act this way, jumping at nothing—at a newspaper! As her heartbeat slowed to normal, she saw the humor in the situation and laughed again, this time meaning it.

The paper was the *Utica Daily Press*. Leaning forward, she held the lamp base closer and made out the date: August 1, 1929. Almost thirteen years ago. A tear at the top cut through the logo and down through a picture of Herbert Hoover smiling at the camera and waving his hat. The headline announced PRESIDENT LEAVES WASHINGTON. Prophetic, although three and a half years early.

Marla decided her foot wasn't really hurt and rose from the bed, bending to retrieve the chimney. The glass was still hot, and rapidly grew hotter when she replaced it on the base, but it was bearable for the few seconds it took to twist the chimney against the clips, making a better seat.

A newspaper . . .

Chiding herself for panicking, and then for her general nervousness, Marla picked up the paper, folded it on the bureau as she moved toward the closet again. Sleep had restored her; she felt well rested. Then she yawned again. Well, a few more hours of sleep wouldn't hurt. By morning she'd be her old self again, ready to face the world.

Suddenly aware of hollow space in the region of her stomach, Marla stopped; then she became aware of other body pressures. Before she did anything else, a trip across the hall was in order. She fumbled for her mules and started to don her robe, then decided she couldn't wait that long. A few minutes later she crossed the hall back to her bedroom, wide awake, with freshly washed face and hands and feeling comfortably cool. No point in going back to bed now. Close the closet door, then take care of hunger.

The napkin-covered tray resembled a tiny mountain range of shadowy bumps in the dark corner of the room. Hunger reiterated its demands by stabbing at her middle, following with a suddden hollow feeling in the back of her throat. For an instant Marla felt nauseated.

The tray . . . no; the food must be spoiled, sitting all day in the heat. Maybe she could raid the kitchen, if she could find it.

She swallowed against the hollow feeling, wiped her mouth, and started to close the closet door. The orange light of the lamp picked out the broken hatbox on the shelf, and her dresses, hanging limp . . .

Something was wrong.

Marla blinked, and stopped in the act of closing the door. The dresses were shoved to the far side of the rod, almost against the wall.

She hadn't left them that way. She distinctly recalled dropping them in the middle of the rod, the handiest place, in her exhaustion. Her last act had been to sweep her hand between them, separating them a few inches in the hope that the worst of the wrinkles would shake out.

Someone had moved the dresses.

Someone had been in the room.

In the closet . . .

Nonsense! You're being silly again, Marla! Stop it, before you dissolve into hysterics—you, the sensible person who picked up the pieces when Dad had his heart attack. Did it darn well, too. The war was the only thing that stopped you from making a go of it.

She remembered watching eyes . . . dirty eyes.

Marla shivered in fright as goose bumps rose on her arms and the back of her neck. It was instinctive, the subconscious reacting in fear to the threat of the unknown, the unknowable. Her conscious mind told her again that there was nothing to be frightened of, but still her body shivered, her teeth chattered softly. She rubbed her wrist, the movement causing the lamp to bounce and the flame to tremble.

Ha. Ha ha. Who's there?

Ohh! She put the lamp on the bureau, and drew her hands down her cheeks, pressure hollowing them. Hunger was forgotten for the moment as she tried to convince herself that her fright was only her imagination working overtime. Why would anyone at Beechhaven want to harm her?

Andrew . . .

You don't even know the boy! You haven't even met him.

He doesn't like me. Reason or not, he threatened me. Remember what he said to Corliss . . .

You didn't hear what he said. You heard Corliss, but you don't know that they were talking about you!

The thought broke loose. She didn't know that

109

it was the boy. At the moment he seemed the logical one to suspect, but suspicion is not grounds for conviction. Not in America. Whatever happened to innocent until proven guilty?

He's been spying on me ...

You think.

I know! Someone has been spying—he came back! He was here while I was sleeping! He moved the dresses because they were in his way!

He! He! He . . . Marla sucked in her breath, losing the argument with herself. Someone was here, yes ... but was it the boy or someone else?

He moved the dresses, insisted her nagging mind.

Did he? I was tired—now I can't remember exactly what I did with them. Maybe I shoved the hangers against the wall myself. I was asleep on my feet, for Lord's sake, maybe I was sleepwalking. They say exhaustion can do that to you, bring on a nervous breakdown, make you hallucinate. Tim and his silly stories—secret panels indeed! I almost think he was trying to scare me.

I do remember! I moved the dresses ... didn't I? *Why* can't I remember?

Marla bit her lower lip until she tasted salt, the pain momentarily overriding the panic that was threatening to capture her again. She would prove that it was all just her own overactive imagination.

Before second thoughts could wilt her resolve, she advanced on the closet, steeling herself; if bogey there was, if someone was spying on her even now, she would face him down, give him something besides a sneak peek behind her back to remember her by!

The small hairs on her neck stood as she stepped into the narrow closet, raising the lamp that she had retrieved from the chest. There was a crawling sensation along her spine, as though even now someone in hiding was watching her . . .

She spun, thrusting the lamp through the door and then back into the bedroom. No one. No one was there.

Marla forced another laugh. She recognized the foolishness of her actions, knew she was behaving like a child passing a lonely cemetery after dark. Whistle, Marla; whistle against the ghosts. No one can hurt you except yourself.

A sudden belch erupted and she clapped hand to mouth in surprise; hunger was insistent, her stomach pressing its demands. The world returned to prosaic normality amid her digestive gases. What was she doing here in this stupid closet? Why was she prowling around at this time of night?

Fears were not forgotten, but suddenly they seemed silly. She was hungry. Go downstairs, find something to eat; your stomach is unsettled— your mysterious spy is only gas. The thought was emphasized by another belch.

But she was here; it would take only a minute to examine the closet walls, to satisfy her suspicions.

The wainscoting surrounded Marla on all sides, broken only by the frame of the door. The crack where the wallboards met the floor seemed tiny, but the painter had been more careful there; in only a few spots was the crack visibly clogged with paint. No help there in finding a secret panel.

Marla scanned the rear wall of the closet, then rapped her knuckles against the boards. The only result was a dull thud, and a self-satisfied smirk came to her face as she moved a few inches farther and repeated the test three more times. The wainscoting was solid; there were no empty spaces to be revealed.

But was that right? There should be empty places between the studs—at least, if wainscoting acted the same as lath and plaster.

Irritated, Marla stepped back into the bedroom and rapped the wall above the wainscoting, repeating the test twice more. Each time, the sound that came back was the same. The test proved nothing, achieved nothing more than a set of sore knuckles.

She sucked at her hand as she stepped into the closet again, then leaned her weight against the wall, pushing in several places. Again, nothing. But would a secret panel reveal itself so easily?

It didn't seem likely. Even secret panels must have latches and hinges. How did it work in the movies? she wondered.

There should be a trigger, something to give when you pressed or turned the right spot or lifted a key. The brass hooks were the most prominent feature. Marla touched the first, tried to jiggle it in her fingers, then tried to turn it. Nothing. She set the lamp on the floor, against the wall, and tried two hooks at the same time, with the same result. Set in the thick coating of paint around their bases, there was no give.

She concentrated on one, brought pressure; pain stabbed through the ball of her thumb, but the hook began to twist, then turned easily. Unscrewing. Marla worked it a few more times until the threads came free of the supporting wood.

The hooks were only hooks. Convinced she was wasting her time, she screwed the hook back into the board, then gave each of the others a briefer test. Nothing happened. There was no secret panel.

She gave up on the hooks, deciding that they were too prominent; if a key existed, it would be better concealed. Rubbing an irritation in the side of her nostril, Marla sniffed. Okay, if a key did exist, what else might serve? The clothes rod?

It was an inch thick, round, and supported on either end by three-inch-square blocks nailed to the walls just beneath wider supports for the shelf. The rod rested in holes drilled through the blocks; the shelf supports were thicker two-by-fours. Beneath the paint, nailheads were visible even in the poor light.

The rod turned freely in her fingers, had less than a quarter-inch play back and forth.

Not the rod.

The hatbox?

Marla giggled as she reached to move the box aside, glad that no one was here to see her in this farce. A cloud of dust stirred into the air . . .

The newspaper. Where did it come from?

The broken box came down in her hands as the question popped into her mind. More dust spilled from the shelf; she sneezed, the eruption violent enough to make the dust motes dance in the thin column of heated air above the lamp, and strong enough to move her back against the doorjamb. Her shoulder blade cracked painfully against the frame.

Marla swallowed against her dry throat, although she had drunk water in the bathroom. It was the dryness of the dust, she told herself. Only the dust.

There had been newspapers tacked to the shelf in the next closet, but this morning only the box was in here. Herbert Hoover had arrived later.

All right! Someone *was* here; someone had moved the dresses. Callie! She did it! It must have been Callie . . .

Why? What would the girl be doing here while you were asleep? Callie's afraid of her own shadow.

"I don't know why!"

The words were almost a shout, and as soon as they were out of her mouth a cricket chirped, astonishingly close. Marla jumped and spun around, heart pounding again. The insect sounded again, and she managed a weak laugh.

A cricket, Marla! Only a cricket.

The sound was steady now; it seemed to come from the area of the bed, a sawing noise that was almost musical as the insect settled into its night routine, serenading its cricket world. In the room's silence the sound was loud.

Perhaps Davis could trap the creature or she could move to another room.

The idea comforted her. She would tell Garman tomorrow that she wanted to change. There shouldn't be any problem, for there were certainly enough rooms.

Torn between relief and heightened nervousness, Marla went back into the closet. The urge to laugh came strongly, but she choked it off. (Only crazy people laugh at nothing.)

Her sanity wasn't in question . . .

(Isn't it?)

She shut out the disturbing thought, refusing to listen to the prodding of her subconscious.

All right, Marla, get this done with. Think: if a secret panel is here, it's well concealed.

If it existed, the chances of finding it tonight seemed slim. (It exists.) The hatbox was still in her hands. She started to put it back, but the box blocked the light from the lamp, and she misjudged, catching it against the edge of the shelf. The board lifted an inch or so.

Click.

Marla froze in mid-move, her breath caught in her throat; then she lowered her head to peer beneath the box. The sound of a latch pulling clear had been faint but unmistakable.

One of the cracks in the wainscoting was perceptibly wider.

Marla lowered the box and the shelf dropped back, the small sound of the board meeting its supports drowning out the noise of the key sliding back and the latch slipping home. The crack in the wall closed.

The movement was unmistakable; she hadn't imagined it.

Marla's hands were suddenly slippery with perspiration. Her heart beat faster with a surge of adrenaline, but this time in excitement. Shifting the box to one hand, she reached to touch the wall. It seemed as solid as ever.

Lift the box, push it against the shelf. *Click.*

Drop the box, let the shelf fall back. *Click.*

There was a panel!

Suddenly Marla tried to do three things simultaneously: one hand holding the box she pushed it against the shelf again while the other hand reached first for the wall panel, then darted in indecision for the lamp on the floor. The box smashed against the edge of the shelf, its ruin completed, shards of brittle cardboard cascading as top and contents spilled. One piece of cardboard struck the corner of her eye, while the old black straw hat in the box bounced off the lamp.

Marla reversed field, grabbing first for the hat and then for the lamp; she missed both. The lamp fell over, the chimney rolling free again while the base rolled against the wainscoting, the wick rubbing against the wood. As the shelf once more dropped against the trigger, the lamp went out.

Damn!

Damn damn damn!

(Marla Doren! Whatever would the Reverend Muthard say?)

Marla ignored the chiding of the shocked censor in her conscience. Damn . . . well, the devil take the Reverend Muthard! At a moment like this, vigorous swearing felt good!

Retrieve the lamp—get rid of the box, dope! Drop it. All right, pick up the lamp and go back to the nightstand for another match—wait: kerosene had spilled from the lamp and wet her hand; better be careful, take another lamp.

The one she found, aided by the moonlight, had no problem with its clips; the chimney stayed put when she replaced it. She went back into the closet, lifted the edge of the shelf, and heard the rasp as the trigger worked, noticeable because she was listening for it. At the same instant, the latch clicked again.

Balancing lamp and raised shelf, Marla pressed on the wall with her foot, and met resistance. Fear was gone from her mind, replaced by frustration. She put the lamp down, raised the shelf again, and pushed with more strength.

The panel swung open on silent hinges as Marla overcame the spring that held it closed. Halfway open, it swung the rest of the way by itself.

Secret panels.

Secret rooms ...

Tim wasn't kidding.

What other surprises did Beechhaven have in store for her? (Corliss; "We're not allowed to tell. That would spoil the fun.")

Spying on people isn't funny!

Marla felt relieved as she picked up the lamp. She wasn't losing her sanity, she hadn't imagined the watcher; he was here, in the closet. He must have retreated through the panel when Skelly knocked at the door.

The memory of the lust that had pervaded the room made her shiver. If for some reason she couldn't move (Alicia upset at the challenge to her schedule), she'd ask Garman to nail the panel shut.

She ducked her head as she stepped through the panel; the top was concealed behind the board that held the hooks. Closed, there was nothing to differentiate it from the wainscoting on either side.

Marla held the lamp high, wishing for her father's five cell flashlight—for anything brighter than this. She made out a room even larger than her bedroom, but so cluttered that it was impossible to pick out the corners. A narrow aisle led away from the panel, moonlight filtering dimly through two windows that were blocked by something bulky. It was a storeroom.

She felt silly. Only a storeroom . . . but what had she expected? Dark dungeons? Dracula?

She moved farther into the aisle, and stepped on paper. She looked down to see another aging newspaper, a classified section. A stack of papers teetered precariously on an old rib-topped trunk. Andrew—the watcher—must have kicked Herbert Hoover into the closet and put him on the shelf, too entranced with his spying to return the paper to the stack.

Watching eyes . . .

The hackles were standing again.

He was behind her . . .

Marla spun, saw only the opening to the closet, the visible rectangle of the bedroom silver in the spill of moonlight. The sensation of being watched was gone again. She expelled held breath, shuddering.

Your imagination! Imagination . . .

(But I'm not tired now. I'm not hallucinating . . .)

Marla rubbed her eyes and blinked rapidly; when she opened her eyes again she caught a gleam, and turned to her left. A marble statue was almost within reach of her hand, its cloth covering slipped far enough to reveal the upper torso of a female nude.

She stared, entranced, her momentary fright forgotten. The statue, perhaps four feet tall, was exquisite in workmanship, and she knew it was very old. Why was it here in the storeroom?

Something so beautiful deserved display. Indeed, why was so valuable an art object here in Beechhaven, the summer house, rather than in New York City?

The apparent vagaries of the Gibsons were beyond her understanding. The very presence of this house proved eccentricity, a trait that was in the genes undoubtedly as much as was the family jawline.

She glanced around, turning away from the closet panel again. The storeroom was jammed everywhere with furniture, trunks, boxes, crates, barrels of every description. One of the barrels near the stack of newspapers must hold crockery; the visible contents were wrapped in newspaper.

Above, a score of chairs hung from the ceiling. Details were hard to discern in the dim light of the lamp, but after a minute Marla thought she recognized some of the furniture styles—that was Chippendale, certainly; and that seemed to be like the Hepplewhite illustrations she had seen recently in a magazine. The construction of the chair was delicate, its beauty apparent even under a coat of dust.

Antiques? It seemed likely. They must be valuable. On the other side of the aisle was a loveseat, almost buried beneath stacks of old magazines.

Marla moved along the aisle, mules scuffing up a cloud of dust—and sneezed again. The sudden sound seemed shockingly loud, and she turned immediately, as though looking to see if she had disturbed anyone.

There . . . is . . . no one . . . watching . . . you!

No one!

She moved more quickly, lamp held even higher as she hurried along the hall, soon reaching the end, where a staircase led down to a blockaded alcove. Two steps down brought her close enough to make out a latch similiar to the one on the closet panel. Another secret entrance? Whose room was on the other side?

She stopped, foot ready to descend another step; she had been ready to spy herself. This was no time to be opening panels into unknown places. Tomorrow, when the children gave her the grand tour, she could identify the room.

Marla backed up the stairs and turned to retrace her path. Here was a pile of luggage—bags and suitcases of every description—and here, resting on top of a pile of boxes, was an open suitcase, divider thrown back to reveal jammed contents, folded canvas.

She stopped, intrigued; the canvas was a painting, folded once to fit in the bag. She unfolded it and saw a portrait of a broad-faced man in a floppy hat and a strange robe. Marla was unimpressed by the dull colors. The edge of the canvas was raw where it had been tacked to the painter's stretcher and perhaps concealed in a frame.

She flipped the painting aside; the one below was smaller, a tortured scene of a sinner suffering in Hell. Marla shuddered, dropped back the painting of the man in the hat, and turned away, but not before noticing that the other side of the suitcase was also stuffed with canvas. The suitcase itself seemed cheap and was heavily scuffed. A strange way to store artwork, but no stranger than the other habits of the Gibsons.

She wondered if any of the paintings were valuable.

Even if not, this storeroom was a treasure room. To have so many beautiful and rare possessions that they could be tossed into storage, helterskelter, without a second thought! It seemed a crime.

Marla knew she was jealous and was not ashamed by the emotion. She started to move on, then a small box near the suitcase caught her eye; it rested just within a cardboard box, with other stuff beneath it. Cloisonné enamel gleamed in the soft light of the lamp.

She steadied the lamp on a carton and pulled the box from its carton; the lid popped up and music began to play. The tune was unfamiliar but pretty. The box was decorated on each side with oval panels, each with a high-wigged lady in low-cut gown or a periwigged gentleman in velvet knee breeches. The people looked as if they had stepped from the wallpaper scenes on the second gallery, but Marla knew instinctively that these characters had been painted in dress, not costume, by a contemporary. The box was very old, and its artisanmaker had created a masterpiece.

If only she could have it for her own . . .

A month's salary wouldn't buy the likes of the music box. Marla sighed again, closing the lid; the tune stopped. The thought of giving monetary value to such beauty seemed crass, greed at its worst. She turned the box over, saw the key on its bottom, and wound it, ready for the next fortunate discoverer. Then she placed it gently back in the carton.

Marla knew she could spend hours examining

the contents of the storeroom, but nausea returned, and her body insisted on attention. She hurried along the aisle, following the tracks of shoes until they stopped halfway along, and then her own marks from that point. . . .

Marla stopped again, staring at the tracks in the dust. The closet panel was still ten feet away, but from this point only the imprint of her mules marked the aisle.

Eight

Impossible . . .

Marla shook her head, not wanting to believe, but the evidence was indisputable. From the stairs at the other end of the aisle to where she stood now, the marks of traffic were heavy; the narrow way was scuffed clean of dust, leaving only an irregular border on either side, which in most cases was only a few inches wide.

Several people had been here recently, or else one person making repeated trips. Marla spotted a single footprint apart from the rest, where someone had stopped and turned away from the general traffic to stand in a gap between two trunks. The print was perhaps a few days old, beginning to fuzz around the edges, and overlaid with a faint, new layer of dust. But it was still clear enough for her to make out a trademark on the heel.

Marla bent, balancing herself with one hand on one of the trunks, the lamp held only inches above the footprint, while she tried to puzzle out the reversed word. (A clue, said a mischievous part of her mind.) The shadows were wrong; she circled the lamp until the light fell at the right angle for her to decipher a backward wolverine.

This print had been made by a man's shoe; certainly it couldn't have been made by a boy—unless Andrew was older than she had assumed, from the overheard conversation. And *if* it was made by Andrew, not someone else altogether. The latter was more likely.

From this point it would be impossible for the makers of any of the footprints along the aisle to reach the secret panel in the closet, unless they could exercise the power of levitation. Climb over the stacks of furniture and barrels? She shook her head; even an acrobat couldn't do it.

Levitation . . . maybe her spy was a ghost.

Marla laughed aloud, the thought patently silly. Then she remembered the mirror trick, and Corliss saying that Gabriel had been an amateur magician—could the trick have been worked with mirrors?

Unlikely. She straightened, a heavy load gone from her mind. They were all only figments of her imagination after all. Her fears had been caused by exhaustion, nerves, and were all for nothing.

There most certainly had been no watching eyes!

Still, Tim hadn't been kidding about the secret panels. Her finding the one in the closet was only a coincidence, although it seemed likely that Garman's father and grandfather had built such nonsense all over the house. The evidence of the storeroom indicated that this one had not been used recently, probably not in years.

Marla moved along the aisle, adding sharp new prints to her earlier trail, and bent to duck through the panel, catching the edge with her fingers to pull it shut. The spring caught suddenly, slamming it the rest of the way and nearly crushing her hand. The sound, as Marla jerked her fingers to safety barely in time, was as loud as a gunshot—further evidence that the panel hadn't been opened recently. The idea that someone had hid in the closet to spy on her proved more ridiculous by the minute.

Still, her mind wasn't satisfied and insisted on answers to the earlier questions: the noise that had awakened her?

Certainly not the panel. Maybe someone had been in the storeroom, but it could have come from someplace else in the house. Or perhaps something in the storeroom fell. It would be easy for one of the precariously positioned stacks to tip over. There seemed little attempt at order, with new additions to the clutter dumped in the handiest position. Marla wondered if Garman was aware of the disorder.

Probably not. Would the master of Beechhaven bother with such a mundane matter as a storeroom, even one filled with antiques? It was more likely that the storeroom fell under Davis's domain. Despite Tim's words, the idea that the man could secretly be irresponsible suited Marla's first impression of him. If the noise had come from the storeroom, likely it was just Davis adding to the clutter.

Her subconscious refused to admit defeat. A strange time for Davis to be about such a chore, wasn't it?

Marla had the effective counter: Yes, but with the shortage of staff, a bothersome trip to the storeroom might well be left until bedtime.

There, Marla! Satisfied?

She spotted her watch, still lying on the bed where she had dropped it in her moment of upset. She picked it up and strapped it to her wrist, surprised to find that no more than twenty minutes had elapsed since she woke.

The dresses? The newspaper?

There were simple explanations for both. The paper was on the shelf all along, Marla decided; she just hadn't noticed it earlier. After all, she hadn't checked the shelf the first time she looked in. It might have come from the stack in the storeroom, but not recently—perhaps it was a leftover from the last time the room had been painted, or even left by the last houseguest, amused by news that now seemed like ancient history.

As for the dresses, at this moment Marla honestly could not remember how she had put them on the rack. Logic told her, after the other evidence, that she must have shoved them against the wall herself. The idea that she hadn't was just her tired memory playing tricks.

Subconscious made a final try: The threat from Andrew?

Were Corliss and the boy really talking about Marla? She didn't know that for sure—she had no proof that the threat was aimed at her. What had they actually said—what had Corliss said?

"You can't hurt her—I won't let you!"

Her. A broad generic term that could mean any female, not even necessarily human. Perhaps the children were talking about one of Corliss's dolls, a pet, or a bird whose chirping annoyed the boy. The possibilities were endless.

126

Of course, none of them put Andrew in a very good light, but Marla now was sure that she had jumped to a conclusion on the basis of what seemed, under light of lucid examination, no evidence at all.

(Are you sure?)

I am sure!

She reached a decision: At the very first opportunity tomorrow, she would confront the boy— no; she would sound out Corliss. Andrew whoever-he-might-be *was* innocent, until proven guilty.

Marla picked up her robe, then changed her mind in the act of tying the belt. She was going to look for something to eat, but would wandering about the house in night clothes be accepted? Probably not by Alicia, perhaps not by Garman. Tomorrow she would sound out Tim on a great many things, including what was and was not acceptable in her personal behavior.

Marla took the robe to the closet, shoving it out of the way to the left—yes, against the wall— then brought the dresses to the center of the rod. Hanging had helped, although pressing would be much better. There must be *something* in the way of ironing appliances, even if only an old iron that had to be heated on the stove.

One of the dresses was new, bought last week in Munger's in Boonville and altered for her by Mrs. Lindner. The frock was bright, a sleeveless, high-collared summer pinafore in quarter-dollar-size red polka dots against white. It took her only a minute to dig fresh underwear and a slip out of her suitcase and change into them. When she came back from the kitchen, she'd finish unpacking before going back to bed.

Two minutes later, Marla's pajamas were folded neatly at the foot of the bed, sheet and coverlet smoothed and straightened to eliminate any mark of her presence. Marla was seated at the dressing table, brushing out her hair. She didn't bother with socks, slipping her bare feet into low shoes.

Satisfied with her appearance even if she should be summoned to another audience with Alicia, Marla picked up the lamp and opened the door—then turned back. The kerosene spill had dried over the base of the other lamp, but she wiped the glass with tissue, then lit it, turning the wick down until it gave just enough light to banish darkness from the room. She placed the lamp on the nightstand, out of the shifting spill of moonlight, its presence a comforting beacon against her return.

She took the other lamp again, adjusting the wick to the point where it gave the most possible light, and went into the corridor. At first the lamp helped her pick her way through the darkness, her shoes clipclopping rapidly as she moved through the corridor. In the back hall, the gloom was only slightly relieved by the row of windows, the moonlight falling over the house at an angle that painted the tulip beds and a narrow strip of lawn silver-white. In that edge, dew sparkled from the sheep-cropped grass.

Marla paused before turning into the corridor that would bring her to the main entrance. Sense told her that the kitchens would be in the back of the house, but sense had had little employment in other aspects of the design. If there was a design. Maybe the stairs at the end of this back corridor would take her directly there. She hesitated. The dining room should be near the main hall. . . . Which way to try?

In that moment of hesitation she glanced through the nearest window and saw a horse-drawn vehicle topping the far knoll: a buggy. It came down the road, carrying no sidelamps, although the tunnel beneath the trees must be pitch dark.

Marla remembered that guests were due, but she couldn't see the occupant or occupants. How many were coming—three or four? With a driver, the buggy couldn't hold that many.

Could the noise that had awakened her have been a train? It seemed unlikely. Trains passing through Lyons Falls could be heard for a long time, their lonesome whistles night-mournful. And the sound of their passage was transmitted through the shelf of granite that underlay most of the village high ground—for that reason, the south end of the village was known as the Rockpatch. Marla had been in junior high before she learned that the street through the Rockpatch had another name.

The buggy reached the bottom of the hill and turned toward the carriage house. A moment later the driver maneuvered the horse around to where the buggy could back into a stall, but the driver did not appear, although Marla could see the horse standing in the traces. If the guests were coming, it was not by this trip of the buggy. She wondered idly what other business could take it out at this time of night.

Hunger prodded again; standing here mooning wasn't finding the kitchen. Eeney, meeney, miney, mo—back the way I know I'll go. Nighttime wasn't the time to explore totally unknown territory. Since the buggy driver was still up, perhaps she'd be lucky enough to find someone to guide her to the kitchen.

Several lamps, gas and kerosene, were lit in the lower hall when Marla came out on the gallery. She glanced back at the mirrored alcove, but there was no mystery now in the night darkness, for a strong light source was needed to enhance the illusion. Glancing ahead, through the bull's-eye she saw the moonlight painting a long path across the lake. Above, the stained-glass skylight was faintly translucent, without passing illumination.

Marla came down the stairs and saw a ruby-shaded lamp burning in Garman's office, but when she looked in, the room was empty.

He must still be up, though. One panel of the front door stood open, a sudden breeze coming into the hall and rippling through the arm opening of her sleeveless dress. As Marla raised her arm to let the breeze caress her flesh, she noticed the glowing coal of a cigarette in the darkness of the porch.

She approached the door. "Mr. Gibson?"

The coal dipped, and a tall figure stepped out of the bulk of a pillar and stood silhouetted against the lawn and the lake.

"Ah, Marla! It is late to be about, is it not? Come, join me in the pleasure of this beautiful evening."

It was Philippe; as he came into the fall of

lamplight from the house, Marla saw that he had changed from the costume of the morning, and now wore a pale V-neck sweater, flannel slacks, and tennis shoes. Apparently he wore no shirt beneath the sweater. The contrast was startling. Out of the formal monkey suit, he seemed much younger, perhaps no older than Tim.

"Monsieur Crateau." She acknowledged his greeting and explained her mission.

"Please, no formalities! You must call me Philippe," he insisted. "Remember, here we are democratic, equals among equals—except, of course, for Madame Gibson. Come, I will lead you through the maze and past the lair of the Minotaur—a cup of chocolate before retiring would not be out of order."

Then he managed a small laugh. "Not as acceptable as a fine cognac, of course. But the madame disapproves of anything with the power to stimulate either flesh or spirit. I sometimes wonder, I must confess, how the madame can accept her share of profits from Gibson Brands, since the division sells nothing nonalcoholic."

Disloyalty in the jester? Marla was amused. Philippe flipped his cigarette into the drive beneath the porte cochere, and started to offer her his arm, but then moved past her, closing the door as she came in. He scooped up a lamp as Marla reclaimed her own, and led her to the room beyond the office, which proved to be the dining room.

It was on a scale with the rest of the house, stretching at least fifty feet toward the rear, high-ceilinged, and almost narrow in proportion. The back wall held two massive gilt-framed mirrors flanking a swinging service door. Either Gabriel or Goulding seemed to have had a thing for mirrors. The light of their lamps bobbed as Marla and Philippe walked in that direction.

The room was paneled with some exotic dark wood, the ceiling holding twin crystal chandeliers ornate with molded plaster and fretwork. Marla's head bobbed as she turned to take in the details, studying the paneling.

"Fruitwood," said Philippe, reading her mind.

"It's beautiful."

"But a mistake, in a house that will be used only one season during the year." He turned back, raising his lamp high and indicating a joining of two panels near the ceiling; they bulged outward. "See? Moisture. It does much damage, spoils everything."

"A shame," said Marla.

"It is impossible to properly heat this house—the tower apartment must be tightly shuttered each autumn, but the walls must be repainted each spring."

The long table in the center of the room was lined with eighteen chairs on each side, but it seemed small for the dimensions of the place. A massive, carved armchair stood at the head of the table; another, much less ornate, was at the foot. The end chairs were upholstered, the side chairs a mixture of styles. Marla recalled those in the storeroom. Perhaps the latter were extras, brought down for large dinner parties.

Across the table, three enormous china cabinets stood against the far wall; ranked closely enough to touch one another, they covered less than a third of the wall space. Oil paintings filled the emptiness, the subjects obscure in the gloom but apparently chosen for size. Each frame was flanked by a pair of candle sconces, the candles uniformly burned down an inch or so.

Along the near wall were two sideboards and a tall chest of drawers between them. Serving and chafing dishes were ranked on the sideboards, awaiting call. Two glass-shaded gas lamps also stood on the sideboards.

Except for a linen runner down the center of the table, and three widely spaced statuary groups along that, the table itself was bare. The groups were Victorian plaster reproductions by John Rogers and seemed out-of-place on the finely crafted table. Marla knew that a Rogers group had at one time been essential to every American parlor—one had been her mother's prized possession, almost her only family treasure. Marla remembered that after her mother died, her father sold the group to a traveling antique buyer whom he met at one of the village bars. That was in 1933, she recalled. Money was very tight—afterward, her father said it was the worst year of the Depression for the lumberyard. After the bank holiday, people fortunate enough to have any money held on to it and would buy nothing that was not absolutely essential.

The Rogers group brought enough money to provide a Christmas for Marla; she still remembered the new winter coat that was her present—her only present. Then a year or so ago she had seen an article on Rogers in the Sunday rotogravure; it said collectors sometimes paid several hundred dollars for some of the choicer groupings.

When she asked her father how much the buyer had paid for her mother's group, he chuckled, remembering how he had talked the man up from eight to twenty dollars. Marla didn't show him the article.

Philippe pushed through the service door, holding it open for her, and Marla found herself in the kitchen, which was as big as the dining room. The long axis crossed that of the dining room, however, making a T. Worktables ran down the center of the room, three of them end to end; the one in the middle was topped with metal. Pots and pans were racked overhead in bewildering array, some of them immense. One iron spider was at least two feet across.

All around were cabinets, the south wall lined with shelves holding canned goods and staples, with bins beneath them; apparently there was no separate pantry. Against the back wall stood three stoves: a massive wood range in the exact center of the wall, and next to it an eight-burner gas range with two big ovens. On the other side, gleaming in pristine white newness, was an electric range, not yet connnected.

Philippe saw Marla eyeing the electric range, and chuckled. "It should not be here, you are right. Bethel had it sent two or three years ago, at a time when she had convinced herself that she could cook. I understand she has no talent at all for the art. It was not until an electrician came to hook it up that Garman was informed the generators could not produce the necessary voltage. So it sits."

"Why didn't he return it?"

He shrugged. "I have not asked, but I would assume he never thought of the matter again."

Beyond the range was a long double sink, a pump mounted on one of the drainboards, although there were faucets as well. Against the short north wall were two gleaming white refrigerators, coil-topped models nearly twenty years old. In front of them was a wooden drop-leaf table, the leaves raised, seven wooden chairs around it, seven places set on the oilcloth cover. Clearly, it was for the servants, but why only seven and not eight?

Philippe, after setting his lamp on the worktable nearest the gas range, went to a massive brass-bound wooden ice box and opened one of the six compartments.

"What is your pleasure, Marla? I prepare an excellent omelet."

Marla protested, "I can fix something myself, Philippe."

"But I insist—after all, I have the reputation of my country to uphold! No other preference? Then an omelet it shall be."

He brought milk and a bowl of eggs, a dish of butter, and other ingredients from another compartment and from scattered shelves. Shunted aside, Marla sat, drawing a high stool to one of the worktables. Philippe lit two of the burners on the range, and then another for the warming oven. Half a quart of milk went into a saucepan, and two minutes later, while the omelet set in the pan, he lit two more burners and began toasting slices of bread in a double wire rack. Before reversing the rack, he added cocoa to the pan of milk.

"Would you like coffee?"

"Chocolate would be fine, thank you."

"Mais oui."

Philippe bustled about energetically, seeming happy as he created an unnecessary amount of work for himself. Soon enough the omelet was ready. Marla brought jam and honey from an indicated cupboard, while he loaded the rest of the now-elaborate meal onto a tray.

"In the absence of the ladies, we have been taking most of our meals on the summer porch."

Carrying the tray, Philippe led the way to a square porchlike room, which Marla hadn't noticed before, off the kitchen a dozen feet away from the stoves. Screened on three sides, the breeze cut across the porch as she followed him through the swinging door. Philippe set the tray on a round table already set with ten places, the plates turned upside down on the red-and-white checked gingham tablecloth. Oilcloth and paper restaurant napkins for the servants, gingham and linen in silver napkin rings for the family . . . democracy at work. The centerpiece of daisies seemed tired.

As Philippe pumped up the gas lamp hanging over the table and lit it, Marla watched with interest; the little wheel was a pump, not meant to be turned. After this she wouldn't be quite so helpless.

"If there are a number of guests," said Philippe, sitting two spaces away from Marla, "dinner is served in the dining room. I prefer the informality of this . . . it is homey, I think is the way you Americans say it."

Marla began to eat. The eating porch was just

over the porch that circled the house; a short distance away she saw the steps zigzagging up to Gabriel's private entrance. Then she heard a horse, but when she looked out she could see nothing of the carriage house or the stables.

Marla decided the omelet was marvelous and told him so after the fifth bite. The compliment pleased him; Philippe preened, eyes sparkling. If only he didn't have that silly mustache . . .

She sipped at the chocolate and nibbled a slice of toast. "Have you been here long?" she asked politely, curiosity burning beyond control. A crumb of toast clung to the side of her hand and she wiped it away with her napkin.

"A few weeks," he said noncommittally.

Marla had the grace to feel embarrassed; his presence was none of her business. Philippe tilted his cup, staring into it, long fingers rolling it until the chocolate was dangerously near spilling.

He decided to say more. "I was in London for more than a year, Marla." He met her eyes. "Before that, I was manager of the Paris office."

"For Gibson International?"

"Yes. Of course, that was only a month before the Boche invaded." His words were bitter, the smile gone from his face. "My family was proud, you understand—achieving such a high position only six years after graduation from the university was an honor. I am still carried on the payroll as manager of the Paris office. Garman promises he will soon find something for me to do to earn my salary. For now, I enjoy an extended holiday."

Marla finished the last bite of omelet. "Forgive

me, Philippe, if I am presumptuous—but why were you wearing formal dress?"

"In France we are still conservative. A manager dresses as a mark of his authority. It is expected. It brings respect. Although I do nothing useful, I wear my authority during the hours of normal employment."

His reasoning seemed suspect—he was in America now and should adapt to the customs of the country. But Marla sensed that his hold to tradition was necessary, a lifeline to the world that had been taken from Philippe by forces beyond his control, the mark of it was more important than ever. Smothering her first temptation to smile, Marla drained her cup.

"But you did get out of the country."

"My family did not."

"Oh. I am sorry, Philippe."

"I have two brothers and two sisters, as well as my parents. I have had no word from them since Paris fell, but I fear matters do not go well for them. You see, my mother is half Jew."

Philippe reached across the space separating them, let his hand fall on Marla's, and managed a smile.

"The war is far away, Marla—we are here, and it is a lovely evening. Perhaps you would honor me, join me in a walk to the lake?"

Marla blushed at the contact, started to withdraw and refuse the invitation . . . then changed her mind. Her inner being was satisfied now that it had been fed; what harm in joining him? Walking was good for the digestion.

(Tim might care)

Tim walked away from me. . . .

"With pleasure, Philippe."

He beamed, and turned out the overhead lamp while Marla gathered the dishes and took them to the sink; he seemed to feel no compulsion to step in there. She debated washing up, and felt guilty when Philippe drew her away. They reclaimed their lamps and left them on the hall table near Garman's office; the latter was still empty.

As soon as they were on the porch, door left open again, Philippe drew out his cigarettes. He offered her one.

"Thank you, no. I don't smoke."

"Sensible. I wish I didn't. Do you mind?"

"So long as it isn't a cigar, not at all."

He produced a lighter, drew deeply, and expelled the smoke with obvious relish, then took her arm to help her down the steps under the porte cochere. Marla wondered if Alicia forbade smoking as well as drinking; she had seen no ashtrays about the house.

The open door behind them was a rectangle of warmth against impenetrable shadows as they moved along the path. The upper portion of the house was painted in moonlight. Fifty feet away, Marla stopped and looked back. The moon was a misshapen reflection in a score or more tower panes, the drapes behind the glass wall drawn almost closed but for a crack no wider than a single pane.

The lawn sloped abruptly, the path becoming steep; it was necessary to concentrate on what she was doing. Soon the boathouse bulked above them, windows blind to the world. Marla wondered which of them guarded the servants—and was Tim behind one of them? No; like herself and Philippe, his status was higher. He was probably somewhere in the house, still sleeping out his exhaustion.

They walked out onto the dock, lake water making small noises as it lapped against the pilings, passing first an oarless rowboat and then a sleek speedster, its highly polished curved decking bright in the moonlight. The rope tying the speedboat to the dock seemed pure white. A ribbed hatch covered the engine compartment, and there were upholstered seats for four in the cockpit.

Marla smiled, suddenly excited. "Oh, Philippe, could we go for a ride? Suddenly I want to feel spray on my face."

"Alas, we cannot; Madame would surely disapprove. The motor would wake her. Skelly will undoubtedly give you a ride tomorrow—the boat is his."

Marla felt shocked; it seemed outrageous that a child so young should have so expensive a toy. Then she appraised her outrage and decided she was jealous. The rich could not be judged by normal criteria, not in matters of their possessions.

"I would suggest a canoe ride," said Philippe. "But I am completely uncoordinated, and a poor swimmer."

Marla laughed with him, and knew as he turned that he was going to kiss her. Her thoughts were jumbled as she raised her face to accept his lips against hers, but her arms hung limp. Philippe broke the kiss; he understood that she had felt no passion. He turned away.

"I am sorry. I had no right to do that."

Anything she could say would seem banal.

Marla moved along the dock, and after a moment he followed, catching her at the foot of the path. They were silent until they reached the break over the steepest part of the slope.

"Philippe, whose boy is Andrew?"

"Andrew? I am sorry, Marla, I do not know him."

"He was with Corliss and Skelly this morning."

"No, that cannot be. There were no visitors today, only yourself. And there are no other children here."

Nine

9:00 A.M.

Marla came slowly awake, rising from a comfortable dream. She wanted to hold it, but it was slipping away—was gone before it became a permanent memory. She sighed, opened her eyes, and stared at the canopy over her head.

Lassitude warmed her body; during the night she had kicked off the covers, and now lay on her back with one foot drawn up against her knee, her left hand brushing the headboard. The room was almost uncomfortably hot as the sun poured its fire over the northeastern United States and southern Canada.

What day was it? The answer came: Thursday. Seventh day of the heat wave. First working day of her new job. Marla blinked, yawned widely, and stretched languidly. This bed was as comfortable as any of the few beds she had experienced in her brief lifetime; much better than the army surplus cot she had cursed in the college dormitory; better even than her own bed at home, with its special comfort that came only with long familiarity. She had slept well.

She turned her head until she could see her watch on the nightstand: nine o'clock now, but seven o'clock suntime; the solar furnace had been spilling its heat against the unprotected planet for nearly two hours.

Nine o'clock!

Marla twisted back, staring in disbelief, and shaking her head to chase the last cobwebs of sleep while the second hand swept off another twelve seconds. Then she scrambled to a sitting position, rubbing sleep grit from one eye while she grabbed the watch with her other hand—please, God, make it wrong! She hadn't overslept the first day of her new job ... please!

Prayer was wasted; the watch seemed to sneer at her as the second hand touched the two, the corner of its distorted mouth bent up in disdain. Despite the constant movement of the second hand, Marla held the watch to her ear, heart sinking as she heard the slow ticking marking off tiny intervals of time and spelling her doom.

Nine o'clock ... what would Alicia think?

Or say?

A few more seconds slipped away, irretrievably lost, while Marla considered her perfidy. Then she scrambled from the bed, grabbing her robe from the footboard, jamming on her mules, and scooping up her toothbrush from the chest in almost the same motion. She left the bedroom door open as she ran across the hall, in her haste not noticing that the sign on the doorknob was reversed. She twisted the knob.

The latch resisted.

Numbed, Marla stared at the offending *Occupied* for a full ten seconds, then turned her head; the doors to the other two bedrooms were closed. Until now there had been no sign of the guests due to arrive last night, nor sound from them, either. Nor sign of Garman, for that matter, when she came back with Philippe, although Marla had spent a good ten minutes in the parlor across from his office, picking out several fairly recent magazines to read.

By one she had been back in bed, but it was almost three before her eyes grew heavy enough to make her turn out the lamp. By then she had relaxed. Despite Philippe's astonishing revelation, Marla had convinced herself that her earlier fears were nothing but her imagination working overtime. Her last conscious thought was a resolution to confront Corliss at the first opportunity this morning, and find out just whom she had been talking to in the attic. Now, as she impatiently looked at her watch again, the same thought filtered back into her mind.

Devil! One of the newcomers must have been assigned to this corridor: the yellow room. (Certainly not the red room!) And almost immediately the door opened, the knob yanked from her fingers. A man stood there, unable to pass until Marla realized she was blocking the way.

"Good-morning, *fraulein*." He smiled, a pronounced accent thickening his words. "You must be my neighbor. I am Ernst Steiner."

"Good-morning." Marla swallowed. "You're German!"

Even as the words slipped out she wanted to recall them, but it was too late. Steiner smiled again, his eyes twinkling with amusement, as Marla colored.

"If German nationality is of itself a crime, I am not guilty, *fraulein*—I am Austrian. Ameri-

144

can now, I am pleased to say. In two more days I shall have been a citizen for three years."

His words were precise, almost too correct, his English from a textbook rather than idiomatic. He was short, barrel-chested, only slighter taller than Marla as they faced each other. In heels, she would tower over him.

"I'm sorry," she said lamely.

He shrugged. "It's nothing. The mistake is natural, considering the present unhappy situation of war. Although your reaction was perhaps unnecessarily forceful—all Germans are not enemies. There are many—refugees—loyal to this country."

Marla's ears flamed again as she accepted his chiding. Steiner was almost as broad as he was tall, graying hair showing sweeps of darkness while his close-clipped mustache was dark with a scattering of gray. His eyes were almost the same color. He was dressed casually, in dark slacks and a pale yellow open-weave sport shirt that revealed too clearly the sleeveless undershirt beneath it. Thick fur showed above the undershirt and in the open neckline of the shirt—even his shoulders were patched with fur.

"Sometimes my mouth opens before my brain starts working," said Marla. "Please forgive me."

"There is nothing to forgive. Impetuousness is a mark of youth, and you need never apologize for being young."

She tried to guess his age: seamed leathery face suggested long years of exposure to the elements, the corded muscles rippling beneath silver-dusted skin told of hard physical labor; but the skin itself seemed surprisingly youthful. In

145

his fifties? At least, she decided. He wore shoes too young for him, wingtips in brown and white, the latter cross-woven for ventilation.

All his clothes seemed too young for him. Despite the apparent bull-strength, Steiner would have seemed better fitted to a business suit, and not out of the way even in Philippe's monkey suit.

"I'm Marla Doren."

"Yes, Garman told me." Steiner smiled again, seeming like a kindly grandfather. "You are here to tutor the children—I wish I had been so fortunate in childhood. But I am preventing you— please, accept my apologies, *fraulein*. We will meet again later, perhaps at breakfast."

He bowed, or nodded—Marla wasn't sure which the dip of chin was meant to be—and moved out of her way. She hurried into the bath, closing the door without waiting to see where he went. The room was steamy from recent use of the tub and hot from the water heater. She turned the latch, perspiring before she could take a fresh washcloth and wet it.

Five minutes later Marla was back in her bedroom, tugging her dress smooth; then she sat on the edge of the bed to roll on fresh nylons, fastening them carefully. She wore the polka-dot dress again this morning, and glanced at her watch as she strapped it in place: 9:12. Time was passing too quickly.

A dozen strokes of the brush would have to do. Marla caught up her hair, fastening it into a prim, businesslike knot to show that the person staring back at her from the mirror was sensible, not inclined to frivolity, and not too young for a position of importance. She inserted bobby pins, debated for five seconds whether or not she should wear a net, and decided against it. Her nails were depressingly dull, but there was no time to buff them now.

There was no sign of Ernst Steiner as she hurried along the back corridor, awash with sunlight, or of anyone else, as Marla went down to the first floor and passed the office.

The sun had not yet moved far enough around to break the gloom of the main hall, and one of the lamps on the sideboard lit the dining room. The table had been cleared of the Rogers groups and was set with a damask cloth and ten place settings clustered near the head. Two heavy, four-branched candelabra had been added, and two bowls of fresh-cut flowers. There was no indication that the settings had been used for breakfast, however, so Marla pushed on into the kitchen.

A buxom, gray-haired woman at one of the worktables turned, staring, her arms dusted with flour; a girl in a maid's uniform peered cautiously around from the sink, where her arms were immersed in dishwater. The maid looked familiar, and Marla decided she must be Callie's sister.

"Good-morning," she said. "Are you Mrs. Davis?"

"Ain't nobody else by that name," the woman said grudgingly.

"I'm sorry I'm late. Is there any chance of breakfast? Coffee and toast would do."

"You ain't late—not 'round here today." She sniffed, working her upper tip against one nostril to fight an itch. "Might as well be runnin' a

147

restaurant. You want juice, here's grapefruit, orange, or t'mata."

"Grapefruit, please."

"Letitia, get the juice. How you want your eggs?"

"One will do. Soft-boiled, if it's not too much trouble."

"What's trouble? All I got t' do in the whole world is stand over a hot stove. Bacon an' sassage on the table. Letitia, you hurry with that juice, an' make up some more toast, y' hear?"

Mrs. Davis dusted her arms and wiped her hands on a towel. Letitia looked around guiltily, then brought a pitcher of juice from the wooden ice box, poured it into a glass, which she placed on a plate, and preceded Marla to the summer porch. Garman and Steiner were already there, with two other men. As Marla reached the door, the one with his back to her straightened, and she recognized Philippe. The fourth man was a stranger.

Marla hesitated at the sight of her employer, feeling her heart sink. But she might as well get it over with, face the music now. She swallowed nervously as she pushed through the door after Letitia, who was turning over a plate across the table from the four men. Although there were ten chairs, there were no places between them.

"Good morning, Mr. Gibson. I'm sorry I'm late."

All four men had been lost in silence, Steiner attacking a plate of sausages while the other three toyed with their coffee. Garman wore suit and vest again, a dark blue pinstripe, and a small-print maroon tie. Marla wondered if he ever gave in to informality.

Against the others, Philippe looked even more foolish in his monkey suit than he had yesterday. Like Steiner, the stranger wore sport clothes; he was a square-faced, blond man, his hair cut so short that his pate had been burned red by the sun. As he looked up, Marla saw a disfiguring scar cut deep across his right cheek. Without it, he would be ruggedly attractive; with it, he was almost frightening.

"Um?" Garman looked up, noticing Marla. "Oh. That's all right, Miss Doren. Did you sleep well?"

"Very well, thank you. It must be the mountain air."

"Miss Hurst worked out a schedule—you'll find it in the playroom. But don't worry about keeping it today. The children will help you settle in after breakfast. I think you'll find them on the tennis court."

A sudden whoop came from somewhere below—Corliss shouting in triumph. Then she laughed. Marla turned around to look out the window, but couldn't see them. When she turned back, Philippe had half risen.

"Good-morning, Marla."

He sat again as she sank into the chair, and then the blond man rose, lifting the silver coffeepot from the alcohol heater. "Coffee?"

"Thank you, yes." She righted her cup and he poured.

"Since no one else will do the honors, permit me to introduce myself. I'm Karl Helmer."

He smiled; he was at least twenty years younger than Steiner, but no older than Garman. Like the Austrian, he was powerfully built, although he was no stockier than Garman.

"Thank you, Mr. Helmer."

"Karl, please . . . Marla."

"Karl." She nodded, sipping her juice; then Letitia returned with the toast. Marla added cream to the coffee, using the silver tongs to transfer a single sugar cube. The setting was elegant, the bone china painted with tiny twining flowers.

"The marmalade is excellent," said Helmer. "Mrs. Davis makes it herself, I'm told."

"A remarkable woman," said Steiner, sourly, staring at the other. Marla was amused by their obvious competition before her.

She glanced at Philippe. Like Garman, he seemed distracted, and had paid her no attention since his greeting. He rolled his cup in his slender fingers as he had done last night. Then he felt the weight of her study and looked up, forcing a smile.

Letitia appeared again, with Marla's egg in a cup. Marla concentrated on her breakfast while Helmer and Steiner chatted toward her and against each other.

"A charming location," said Helmer, glancing out the windows. There was no trace of accent, but Marla wondered if, like Steiner, he was Austrian. "I wouldn't mind making my home in these mountains."

That brought Garman to life. He blinked, then stared at Helmer for several seconds, eyes hooded. Then he stood and tossed down his napkin.

"I have work to do."

Philippe scraped back his chair, cup clattering as it nearly fell against his saucer, and stood with him. Steiner looked toward his host.

"You will be in the office?"

"Yes." The word was almost a snap; then he was gone, Philippe following in a hurry.

Marla thought Garman's behavior astonishing, but neither of the others remarked on it. Helmer poured more coffee for himself, Marla refusing his offer. She hurried with her breakfast, giving them answers as often as seemed necessary. Then she was done, smiling at both as she stood and excused herself and went into the kitchen.

"Mrs. Davis!" The cook looked up from the pie crust she was rolling. "Is there a back door?"

"Service stairs through there." She jerked a thumb toward a door in the north wall. "Take you up or down, whichever you're a mind t'. Letitia, you go get the rest o' them dirty dishes. Go on, girl! Stop gawkin'."

Letitia scooted to obey, ducking out of Marla's path; the girl's eyes remained on Marla as she backed around her, and then she was almost running for the porch, seeming as frightened as her sister had seemed yesterday. Marla turned to watch her, and then the service door swung in and a brown-haired young man came through, rubbing tousled hair and arching his neck. He saw Marla and stopped.

"Well, hello!"

"What do you want, Jack?" demanded Mrs. Davis.

"Just some of your marvelous coffee, Liz," said

the youth. "You wouldn't begrudge that much to a man with a broken back, would you?"

She sniffed, then turned back to trimming her crust. This must be the college-boy helper, Marla decided. She had expected a boy, but he seemed as old as herself. In the same moment, a sour thought slipped out: Why wasn't he in the service?

"Corliss said you were a looker," he said, "but she didn't say the half of it. I'm Jack Franklin, and you, of course, are the beauteous Marla Doren."

"Beauteous?" she questioned, smiling.

"Beautiful beyond beauty, beautiful in every way. I wouldst kiss thy hand, sweet princess, but I'd get pine tar all over thine alabaster skin."

He held out his hand and she saw the black smear. "Jack-of-all-work, that's me."

Mrs. Davis snorted, and he drew back, one hand dramatically against his breast. "Ah, the slings and arrows of misfortune have brought me low!"

Marla laughed. "I don't think the quote is correct."

"Who cares?" Jack shrugged. "I'm glad you're here, teacher. Prospects for this summer seemed dreary indeed without human company."

"Beechhaven isn't underpopulated."

"But none of them qualify—they're either too old or too young. Except for you, sweet princess."

"You come for coffee or t' sweet-talk?" demanded Mrs. Davis. "You better get a move on, Jack, 'fore Cassini comes hollerin' again."

"The slavey's work is never done," said Jack,

sighing. "Until this evening, fair one! My heart shall ache with longing."

He drew back again, forearm against forehead, then turned away, head hanging low while he slunk to the sink and brought a heavy mug from the sideboard. Marla laughed. Mrs. Davis scowled, then the frown broke, although she succeeded in fighting off the temptation to laugh. Marla read the message in her eyes as she headed for the stairs, and knew that Jack played the fool just for her.

The stairs brought her to a storage room behind the porch, the walls studded with hooks and hung with garden equipment; there were also three lawnmowers, a lawn roller, and half a dozen coiled garden hoses. The porch itself was stacked with empty cartons and two small ice boxes, the top of one open to reveal a pool of water but no ice. There were two or three old chairs, one of which was a weathered backless rocker, and a screen door at the very end, where the porch turned to start the climb back up the side of the house, or let her down three unpainted and rickety wooden steps.

The image was not in keeping with the rest of the house, and the middle step sagged alarmingly as it took her weight. Marla hurried down, relieved to be on the ground, and paused to look up at the side of the house. It towered above her, immense as she stood close to it; neck aching as she bent her head back until she could see the line of sky. She let her eyes travel along the roofline until she saw one of the bogeys, a lumpish shape peering over the edge as though it was staring at her.

Watching eyes? If there were any, they were as inanimate as the stone kings!

Corliss yelled again, in triumph, her voice coming from the cluster of buildings at the bottom of the knoll. Marla moved in that direction, swerving to pass one of the sheep; the animal's eyes followed her, although it never looked up from its browse. Then as she dropped far enough for the lawn to the south side to come into view, she saw a stooped figure moving through the flower beds. The old floppy hat tilted back, and Marla knew he was looking at her, his busy hands still for the moment. But he said nothing as she crossed the path through the tulips and went on down the knoll.

Jack Franklin's words came back; so she was the only attractive young female. The thought made her smile. There certainly was no shortage of young men! There were at least three for her to choose among: Tim, Philippe, and now Jack. It was almost an embarrassment of riches.

The voices of the children grew louder as she approached the carriage house and glanced in curiously. There was the brightly colored hotel wagon, and in the stall next to it was the buggy. Then Davis popped into view, startling her. She slowed.

"Good-morning."

He stared, without blinking, then nodded. "Mornin'."

"Where are the tennis courts?"

He jerked a thumb. "Out back."

Marla broke from her trance; that wasn't what she had intended to say! Why did the man make her so nervous?

Why was he watching her now?

She shuddered as she turned the corner of the building. The spell broke as she saw the children, Skelly chasing a ball he couldn't reach.

"Match!" called Corliss. "You owe me another—"

She saw Marla and broke off whatever she had been going to say. "Hi! Want to play a set?"

The children were dressed in outfits similar to yesterday's, but now they wore tennis shoes. Marla smiled. "Later, perhaps. Who's ahead?"

"Oh, I am. Although Skelly's getting better," Corliss conceded. "He beat me twice this morning, but I got him four times so far."

Skelly followed his sister to the sideline, staring without blinking as his eyes met Marla's. The boy's face was expressionless, and she glanced quickly at the girl again. Like Davis, Skelly made her nervous.

"Perhaps I should play Skelly first," she said lightly. "I'm way out of practice—I haven't been on a court in ages."

"If Tim would come out we could play doubles. Boys against the girls."

"All right, Corliss—you take on Tim and I'll take Skelly. But right now you two are supposed to be showing me the house. How about it?"

"Sure. Come on, Skelly."

The boy picked up a press while Corliss gathered up the balls they had been using, and Marla waited until the equipment had been carried to a locker just inside the first stall of the carriage house. Then Corliss skipped ahead, Skelly walking beside Marla and glancing at her every few steps. Still nervous, Marla let her hand

155

drop to Skelly's shoulder; she expected him to shrug away, but instead he matched his pace to hers, stretching his short legs a little farther each time.

The concession pleased her; maybe there would be no adjustment problems after all.

"I understand the speedboat is yours, Skelly. Perhaps you'll give me a ride later?"

"If you like," he said softly.

"I'd like it very much."

He smiled, looking up, his face suddenly angelic. "Why can't we go to the island? We could take a picnic lunch."

"Hey, swell!" said Corliss. "You ask Liz, Skelly—she likes you better than me." Then she glanced at Marla. "That is, if it's okay with you, Miss Doren."

"A picnic sounds like fun." That was something else that there'd been no opportunity to do this year. "Okay, it's settled. Skelly, you go ask Mrs. Davis. We'll meet you upstairs."

The boy dashed ahead to the entrance on the north side, while Corliss led Marla to another screen door at the south end of the house, and from there to a side entrance offset a dozen feet from the front corner. Marla found herself at the foot of another staircase, the hall at the top running toward the back of the house.

"This is Mother's room," said the girl, indicating a corner room. "Both these doors are hers. This third door is Father's sitting room." It was well back from the first two. "Between them, they have the whole side of the house. Skelly's room and mine are through here."

She opened another door, into a sealed corridor, relieved of darkness from light coming from the open door to a bedroom. Corliss stood in the doorway and Marla looked in at what was obviously a designer's idea of a boy's room. It was large and airy, three big windows looking over the porch and down to the lake. There were Indian rugs on the floor, an Indian blanket on the bunk beds, and college pennants on the walls. A long desk-worktable in front of the windows bore a partly built model airplane, while several other models were suspended on thread from the ceiling.

There was a mirrored double dresser, and a closet standing open to reveal a rank of clothing on hangers; but except for the unfinished model on the table, there was no evidence that a boy actually lived here. Everything was neatly arranged, too neatly; it was a photographer's set.

Corliss moved on, passing another door. "That's the playroom—really it's the nursery, but don't ever say that in front of Skelly!" She giggled. "Here's my room."

Like her brother's, Corliss's bedroom was carefully arranged; but everywhere was the mark of the girl's personality—stuffed animals and dolls spilling over the chest and the four-poster bed, and ruffles everywhere. The closet was closed, but Marla knew it would be untidy. This room was lived in.

"It's very nice, Corliss. Much nicer than my room at home."

Was that jealousy tinging her voice? Marla felt ashamed, but the girl took no note of her tone. Her room and Skelly's were exactly the same in dimension, but Corliss's was much more cluttered, although each piece of furniture was matched by its equal down the hall.

Corliss backed out of the room and led the way back to the playroom-nursery. It proved as large as the bedrooms. There were twin desks before the windows and a large cork bulletin board against one wall; a small blackboard was on the other side of the room, while shelves lined all three walls. Half the shelves were given over to books, the rest to playthings.

"This is where we have to study," said Corliss, wrinkling her nose. "Dumb."

Marla smiled. "You don't like studying?"

"Oh, it's okay, in the wintertime. But we have to do it all year round, and that's not fair."

"An hour a day doesn't seem so terrible," said Marla. She settled into a comfortable armchair, crossing her legs. "This is a very nice room too, Corliss. . . . Tell me—who is Andrew?"

Marla was prepared for almost any reaction except the one her question produced. Corliss spun, staring, her face turning almost white, her mouth open. She started to say something, then jerked around, ran to the door, and peered into the hall. Then she closed the door and leaned against it.

"Where did you hear that name?"

The child was trembling. Marla rose from the chair and placed her hand on Corliss's shoulder.

"What is it, Corliss? What's wrong?"

Corliss shook her head. "You must never speak that name! Please, Miss Doren! Promise me you won't!"

Ten

The child's face mirrored Marla's own as it had
been yesterday, and the memory of unknowing
fear washed back across Marla, chilling her
spine. The change was shocking—the bright in-
quisitive youngster replaced by a frightened little
girl.

Marla swallowed, and drew Corliss closer, holding her for a moment in reassurance. The child
pressed her face to Marla's side, and she could
feel the fluttering of the girl's heart transmitted
to her own. Then she lifted Corliss's chin and
made her look up.

"What is it, Corliss? Who is Andrew?"

"No!" She whimpered. "Don't say his name!"

"What has he done to frighten you so?"

"Nothing! Nothing . . ."

Corliss squeezed Marla tightly, shivering.
"Please, don't ask me about him."

The girl's fright was almost palpable in the at-
mosphere of the playroom. Marla drew a shallow
breath; as it had yesterday, the temperature
seemed suddenly cooler. She turned her head to
the window, but the sun was bright outside, not
obscured by clouds.

Her eyes flicked around the room, then rose reluctantly to the ceiling. Whoever Andrew might be, Corliss's fright was real. Marla spoke softly, almost whispering.

"Corliss, I won't mention . . . *him* again. I promise."

The child held Marla tightly for a moment longer, then looked up, studying her face. Marla could feel the pace of Corliss's heart slowing to normal. Then the girl pulled away to look out the window, Marla three paces behind her.

"If you ever want to talk about it . . ."

The shake of her head came swiftly, cutting off the phrase before Marla could finish. Where had the laughter gone? The transformation in personality was complete: this child was a stranger to the Corliss of a few minutes ago. She sat at one of the desks, hands folded, staring out the window. Moving closer, Marla could see the tiny tremble in her wrists. Another minute dragged in silence before the trembling eased, and Corliss sighed, turning her head to look up at Marla. She bit her lip, her voice small when she finally spoke.

"I can't. You must believe me." She sniffed, and wiped the corner of her eye. "I'm sorry, really I am. You must understand."

"I do. But remember, Corliss: I want to be your friend. Not just a friend with whom you can play games, but a real friend. If you ever do want to talk . . . talk about anything at all . . . you can come to me."

The girl nodded, and Marla forced a smile that she didn't feel. "Now, how about showing me that fabulous ballroom?"

Corliss started to wipe her hand across her nose, then thought better of it and opened a desk drawer to bring out a tissue. She blew her nose and wiped away the tears staining her cheeks, then went to the door; her face was still pale, but her eyes seemed brighter, almost back to normal.

Marla followed Corliss through the hall and down the other corridor, stopping at what seemed a cul-de-sac across from the door to Garman's sitting room. Recessed about eighteen inches, twin panels ran from floor to ceiling, heavily scrolled. Two electric fixtures were on the walls of the alcove, gallery lamps that could be focused on the panels.

Then Corliss turned a decoration that proved to be a recessed knob, and the entire wall opened inward. The panels were two wings of a massive door, each nearly five feet wide. The weight of the panels must be tremendous, but, counterbalanced, they swung on silent hinges.

The light from the window at the end of the hall was not sufficient to penetrate the darkness of the room revealed by the opening of the great door. Corliss reached around the door and drew out a taper longer than her own arm; lighting it, she moved along the near wall, touching the flame to candles in high sconces across the room.

Marla moved into the ballroom, astonishment growing; after the tower, she thought she was beyond astonishment. The corridor ceiling was perhaps nine feet high, but the ceiling in this room was eighteen or twenty feet above the floor. The room stretched at least sixty feet across to the far wall—all the way to the back of the house—although even that wall was unbroken by windows. Narrow mirrors in gilt frames—mirrors again!—marched around all four walls, almost touching, the bottom of the frames beginning at the middle of the walls and extending to the ceiling. The sconces were more than a foot below the mirrors.

It was impossible to see the mirrors up close, but Marla's ghostly image was repeated endlessly across the mirrors just barely tilted inward.

"Do you like it?"

Corliss whispered the question shyly, coming back with the taper after bringing a score of the flickering candles to life. Marla turned and turned again, breathing softly, almost afraid to speak.

"It's lovely, Corliss!"

At the rear was a small stage, almost lost in the shadows; overhead, six great chandeliers marched in two rows beneath the ceiling. The slight breeze created by Marla's and Corliss's movements was enough to start tiny crystals tinkling, the sound so faint that at first Marla was not sure she heard it. Then she moved farther, and the tinkling began again.

Now she saw the squares of the chessboard, dark and light barely a contrast in the dim light of the room, arranged in the mathematical center of the parquet floor; each square measured a yard on each side. It took eight of her longest paces from the entrance to reach the first row; she stood on the border of the game board, visualizing the living pieces moving to the command of laughing guests.

Incredible! Something like this belonged in the castles of Europe, or the New York and Newport playhouses of nineteenth-century millionaires.

But that was what Beechhaven was: a playhouse for two generations of Gibsons.

"It's beautiful, Corliss!" she whispered. "If I close my eyes I can almost see the beautiful ladies and grand gentlemen. Listen—hear the music?"

The echo of long-ago orchestras filled the air around her, the mirrors reflecting swirling ball gowns and stiff-collared tuxedos, all stored now in trunks and choked with mothballs, the wearers aged and gone to their graves. Marla sighed, and Corliss did the same.

"This is my favorite room. I wish I lived here when Grandmother was young and had her parties. For my wedding I want a grand ball just like the ones she told me about, and I want it right here."

Corliss lifted imaginary skirts and began to move, pirouetting and bowing to an unseen but apparently appreciative audience. The child's fright seemed gone, evaporated in her dreams of grand life. Again Marla listened closely and could hear the strains of music echoing from the tinkling of the crystals, music embedded in the fabric of the room about them: Strauss waltzes, *The Merry Widow*, the laughter of young people, beautiful women and handsome men. She closed her eyes, and they came to life, vibrant ghosts—

"What are you two doing?"

Yesterday vanished, the bubble of imagined memories burst by Skelly's voice. The boy stood in the great doorway, looking at them. Corliss looked up at Marla, smiling a secret smile; they shared guilt at being caught in the same dream, but they shared something more . . . something special. Something no boy could ever know.

Suddenly a giggle burst from Corliss and she ran to her brother. The spell was broken—both spells . . . all ghosts vanished, friendly and malignant. There was only imagination, the minds of child and adult pretending. Dreams vanished, and what remained was prosaic fact, the dull world of the everyday. Marla sighed regretfully.

But the mystery of Andrew remained.

She blinked, brought back to reality. Corliss's fright had not been pretended: the boy must have threatened her. Very well; she would attack the problem of Andrew from another direction: go to Garman—no; go to Tim first. She would be more comfortable sounding him out. (Philippe doesn't know the boy, and he's been here only a few weeks, but Tim has been here nearly two years.)

Andrew must have come from another house; Marla wondered how close the nearest neighbor was. And where was Tim this morning? He couldn't still be sleeping.

"What did Liz say?" demanded Corliss. "Will she do it?"

Skelly smiled disdainfully. "Of course. The basket will be ready in half an hour."

Corliss clapped her hands. "Good! She'll do anything for you, Skelly. She'd make me go to Father, and he'd tell me to stop bothering her while she was busy. She's always busy! Did you tell Father?"

Skelly shook his head. "I tried, but he has those men in the office. As soon as they saw me they chased me away and closed the door."

The look on his face said clearly that he considered the exclusion an insult.

Corliss turned back to Marla. "You'll have to tell him before we go—Father has to know whenever we leave the grounds. Otherwise he'd worry about kidnappers."

To Marla the idea seemed like something out of pulp fiction. Kidnapping didn't happen anymore, not since the Lindbergh case.

"Has anyone ever tried to kidnap you?"

"Once, when we were real little," said Corliss. "I don't remember what happened, but they didn't get away with it—I guess Mother screamed and brought help. Ever since, we've had a bodyguard, but Sam Keasbey was drafted just before we came up here. Father said if we were going to be safe anywhere it would be here."

Suddenly Marla felt a little less envious of the Gibson wealth, of the material possessions surrounding them. What point in having great riches if you couldn't allow your children to walk the streets, knowing they were safe?

She thought of the newcomers: Helmer could be a kidnapper, with that scar on his face. He certainly looked the part of a desperate man. The thought amused her. Steiner could fit the pattern too; their demands were the reason that Garman and Philippe had seemed so distracted this morning.

The thought was silly; she put it out of her mind. "We still have half an hour—what else do you have to show me this morning?"

Corliss cocked her head. "If we're going to go crawling around the island, you better change your clothes. Do you have any slacks?"

Marla said yes, glad she'd put a pair into her suitcase, almost as an afterthought; she had been sure that there would be no opportunity to wear them.

"Are you sure your grandmother won't object?"

"Mother would, but not Grandmother—not to wear on the island. The last time she came with us she wore an old pair of Grandfather's trousers. If you have them, you better put on tennis shoes too. Leather soles are no good for climbing on the rocks."

Marla could not picture the carefully sculpted Alicia Gibson in trousers, nor imagine her clambering around on rocks. She smiled.

"I thought your grandmother was confined to her tower."

"Oh, she could come down if she wanted to. She just stays there since she and Mother had their big fight."

Marla's curiosity got the better of her, and the question slipped out before she could stop it: "And when was that?"

"Last year, just before we left New York to come up here. Boy! You could hear the screaming all the way on the other side of the apartment, with the whole building between them and us."

Corliss giggled again. "Now they won't even ride on the same train. Grandmother comes up first, and Father has to send the special car back for Mother. Georgette has to come in twice a week to do their hair—Tuesdays for Grandmother, and Thursday for Mother."

"Your mother is ill, though, isn't she?"

Corliss shrugged, looking at her brother before she answered, "She says she is."

"Mother wasn't going to come up this summer," volunteered Skelly, "but Father insisted. She wanted to spend the summer with some friends in Newport."

It was the longest speech Marla had heard him make. He smiled, his cherubic features almost too angelic, and she decided he was loosening up toward her. His initial reluctance to talk must have only been shyness.

Marla returned the smile, although uncomfortably aware that she was talking about her employer's wife. "It's a good thing this house is so big."

"It isn't big enough," said Corliss cynically. "Not for the two of them—Buckingham Palace wouldn't be big enough. Skelly, you put out the candles."

"Okay. I'm gonna bring my swimsuit, Corliss."

His sister looked at him; Marla was sure Corliss's eyes narrowed, searching his expression. Was something hidden in his meaning?

Corliss shrugged. "Okay. I'll bring mine too. The water is nice and warm now, Miss Doren."

"I'll join you," said Marla. A swim would be refreshing—another activity that there had been no opportunity for her to enjoy this year.

Skelly opened a recess in the wall just within the door and brought out a candlesnuffer taller than himself; he started along the wall, ghost fires dying across the room with each pace. Soon the ballroom was in darkness again.

"I better catch your father now," said Marla. Before he saw her in slacks. "Is there a shortcut from here?"

"There is to the back of the house," said Corliss. "But you have to go through Father's rooms, and he doesn't like that."

"All right. Where will you two be?"

"Out front," said Corliss.

Marla left them to close the ballroom, eyeing Bethel's rooms as she passed them. She wondered what their mother was like. Then the first door opened and Callie popped out, carrying a pail of soapy water, a feather duster tucked under her arm. She saw Marla and jumped.

"Oh!"

"Good morning, Callie." Marla smiled.

"M-mornin', miss!" The girl backed away, then turned so quickly that water sloshed out of the bucket, wetting her skirt. Aghast, Callie stopped; but none of it had touched the floor. She scurried down the stairs.

The girl obviously was petrified. Marla studied the closed door to Bethel's room as she followed Callie more slowly. Her image of Bethel was taking form around the conviction that she was an unpleasant person. Marla wondered what had been the cause of the argument with her mother-in-law.

The affair was none of hers. She went out onto the porch, rounded the corner, and saw Davis and his wife standing close together. They shot a look in her direction; their conversation had stopped at the sound of her footsteps. She nodded to them, but the hard anger in their faces did not soften.

Marla was twenty feet beyond them when Mrs. Davis spoke. "Miss Doren, you mind yourself today, you hear?"

"What?" Marla spun. "I'm sorry—what did you say?"

"You be careful, that's all. You watch that girl."

"Liz—"

"Shut your trap, Oren!" she said, turning on her husband. "You spoke up when you should of, there'd be none o' this trouble now!"

She was finished; she stomped off down the porch and turned the corner. Amazed, Marla stared after the woman.

Davis sighed. "Miss Doren, you pay no mind to Liz. She thinks Corliss has been playin' tricks on her, stealin' food an' the like. She ain't, but I can't make Liz see it."

No wonder Corliss had sent Skelly to beg the picnic lunch. Marla nodded. "I understand; don't worry."

"Liz has been havin' woman troubles, you know. She's been actin' half crazy ever since the family come up for the summer."

"Have you taken her to a doctor?"

He shook his head. "She won't go. She don't trust the likes."

Marla felt sorry for the man; her earlier suspicions of his motives disappeared. He seemed pathetic, a man on the verge of old age, unable to understand what was happening to him. His wife must be making life hell for him—probably she was the one responsible for turning the work girls into scared rabbits. All Davis had left was his pleasure in the *Queen of the Lakes*. Suddenly Marla was sure that his wife had been miserable yesterday, which was why he had taken the colorful wagon to meet the train.

169

"If I can do anything . . ."

Davis shrugged and turned away without saying more. Marla watched him go, aware that life could turn against others as much as it had against her own peaceful world.

She sighed, moving toward the main door again, which was standing open—and nearly bumped into Jack Franklin as he stepped out.

"Oh! Jack, you startled me!"

"Well, hello again." He grinned, his hand grasping her arm. "Very much hello, Marla."

He came out, maneuvering Marla before him and out of line of sight of the hall. As with Philippe last night, she knew he was going to kiss her.

"Don't, Jack," she said quietly. "Don't do anything we'll both regret."

"I'll have no regrets," he said. But he read the message in her eyes, released her arm, and backed off. "Scrap 'Operation Assault'—you're not the type." He laughed. "My mistake. I thought I read you differently, Marla. Let's start over again, okay?"

"Let's not."

He shrugged. "Okay. But it's going to be a long summer, beautiful one. When you get tired of Frenchie, remember me."

He turned away, jumping from the porte cochere to lope down the path toward the boathouse. Marla stared after him, fingering the spot on her arm touched by his strong fingers, and knowing that he had seen Philippe kiss her last night.

Strike one name from her list of eligibles: that still left two. Philippe might be the sort of man who grew on you, who aged well. And Tim . . .

Her mind shied away from thinking about Tim.

Marla turned into the house, thoughtful, still rubbing her arm as she came abreast of the office. The door was open now, and there was no sign of Steiner and Helmer; Garman was at his desk, studying papers. No; he was staring at the papers without seeing them.

"Mr. Gibson?"

He jumped, his face white; then he looked around and saw Marla, and gained a measure of control. "Yes, Miss Doren? What is it?"

Marla told him about the picnic, and he nodded. "Fine. I'm almost tempted to join you myself."

"Why don't you?" she asked. "It's a beautiful day."

He forced a smile. "Be gone, Satan! Oh, Tim! Are you ready to go?"

Marla turned; Tim had come up behind her, so silently that she hadn't heard him. He was dressed in a suit, but he seemed younger than he had yesterday, the dark circles gone from beneath his eyes.

"Good-morning, Marla. I'm ready, Garman."

"Davis is bringing the rig. I want you to jump on those people—if necessary, buy the damned company! I want this phone working today!"

Tim grinned. "If pressure can do it, they'll have a crew out here this afternoon."

"Here are the calls I want you to make this morning." Garman picked up several sheets of yellow pad paper, folded in thirds, as Tim came in to take them. "I want answers from Morris and Graham, so wait for them. From Llewellyn, too, if you can track down the slippery SOB."

"Will do. I'll light a fire under all of them." He glanced at his watch, a gesture Marla emulated; it was just past ten. "I'll be back for dinner, one way or another."

"Good." Garman sighed. "God, but I'm tempted to head back to New York, no matter—"

Realizing that Marla was still standing there, he cut off whatever he had been about to say. "Is there anything else, Miss Doren?"

She shook her head. "No. Excuse me . . ."

As Marla backed away toward the office stairs, Tim caught her arm.

"Are you feeling better today?"

"Much better, thank you. Tim, I want to ask you—"

"Not now, Marla; I haven't time. Tonight, if I do get back in time for dinner. If not, then we'll talk the first chance we get. I have things I want to say myself . . . things I should have said four years ago."

Oh, Lord! He was going to kiss her too!

But Tim only held her arm for a few seconds, their eyes meeting, something smoldering deep within each of them. Then she pulled away and ran for the back of the house. Her feet dragged, and when she reached the landing she paused to search out the photograph of the three boys. One of the boys was Garman, she was sure; but who were the other two?

The youngest boy again captured her; he seemed about to speak. Marla stared until she realized she was holding her breath, then broke away, hurrying through the illusion and on up to her room.

Five minutes later she crossed the back of the

house, swimsuit wrapped in a towel, and took the service stairs down to the kitchen. All three of the maids were there now, lined up before Liz, who stood, glaring, arms akimbo. She shot an angry glance at Marla.

"I came for the picnic basket," said Marla.

"Skelly has it," she snapped.

"Oh. Okay." Marla turned away, then stopped. "Liz . . . does Garman have any brothers?"

"Huh?" The question startled her. "Sure, George—he's the youngest. The Germans got him interned in Germany."

"That's all, just the one?"

"All that's livin'. There was Gabriel, he was the oldest, but he died a long time ago when he was just a kid. Drowned, out there in the lake."

"Oh." Now she was sure that the three boys in the photograph were Garman and his brothers; Garman appeared to be no more than a year younger than the dead Gabriel. "Thank you, Liz."

"For what? Just you remember what I tol' you, miss—keep your eye on that Corliss, 'fore she does somethin' sneaky. You watch her!"

Marla felt sorry for Corliss as she made her way back through the house. It must be terrible to live in a house filled with so many cross-currents of hatred: mother against grandmother, servants against one another. The strange look in Tim's eyes yesterday came back to her—perhaps he did hate his employer. But if that was true, why stay here? Tim was independent and could go anywhere he wanted.

For that matter, why did Garman insist that his wife come here when there was so much animosity between her and Alicia? Marla could see

173

no sense in forcing a continuation of their strife; he could only increase Bethel's resentment against himself as well as his mother.

Hatred . . . could emotions become a part of the structure of a house? Could a house take on life of its own, feeding off anger and distrust, until it was able to force its emotional orientation upon the inhabitants? Some houses were happy places, the people living in them content even through normal misfortunes. Others seemed to breed discontent, even evil. . . .

The thought made her shudder, and she forced it away as she hurried out onto the porch. A glance into the office showed it empty; perhaps Garman had joined his guests, Helmer and Steiner.

The porch was empty. Marla looked around, then heard Corliss calling her. The children were already on the dock, Skelly loosening the rear tie of his boat—the stern, Marla reminded herself. Undoubtedly he was very nautical about the matter.

A brisk breeze had sprung up, bringing with it the smell of the pine forest, and over it the fainter odor of smoke. The sky to the north was hazy, the breeze coming from that direction to make choppy little waves across the lake.

"There's a forest fire someplace," said Corliss when Marla sniffed. "I hope it doesn't come this way."

"How far away is it?" asked Marla.

"I don't know," said the girl. "Skelly, try the radio."

The boy brought a portable radio up from beneath the dash and turned it on; it warmed

174

while he finished untying the speedboat from the dock, Corliss helping Marla step down into the cockpit. Then the radio began to crackle and spit. He tuned it across the band, without luck.

"Nothing. Reception is lousy up here," he said, looking at Marla. "Sometimes I can get WIBX, but even the big antenna up at the house doesn't do much good."

He turned his attention to the engine, which stuttered once, then coughed and roared into life. Water was churned into white froth behind them as he moved the boat away from the dock, expertly, and increased the speed. Spray was flying into Marla's face as they headed into the wind; laughing, she held her hair.

The island loomed before them, Skelly heading the boat along the south side, and at last Marla saw that it was separate from the distant land. The island was shaped something like South America, the Horn being the projection pointing toward the house. In the middle rose twin hills about five hundred feet high; both were heavily forested with towering first-growth pines.

The shore along the south was a projection of rocks that offered no harbor. Skelly steered around the far end of the island, which curved more gently and was dotted with tiny coves. He slowed the speed, drifting past the first two, then brought the boat into the third cove, easing it to a stop beside a rickety old dock. A tottering bathhouse was at the end of the dock.

Skelly tied up. "I'm going to change," said Corliss, jumping onto the dock, which was only two feet above the waterline. "I want to swim."

"Oh dear!" Marla said suddenly. "I don't have a cap."

"There's some in the bathhouse," said Corliss. "Come on, Skelly! Last one in the water has to clean up the mess after lunch."

Skelly ran after his sister, dock shaking beneath his pounding feet. Marla followed, at a more leisurely pace, and five minutes later came out to see them already splashing about in the water.

"Jump off the dock, Marla!" called Corliss.

"No, thank you!" She eyed the rocky beach, and picked her way carefully, wincing as sharp rocks cut into the soles of her feet. Then she waded into the water, sighing with pleasure as it came high enough to permit her to turn on her back and float. The bouyant water carried her along. . . .

Tightening face warned Marla that she was beginning to burn. She heard the children splashing as she turned over, beat her way back to shore, and made her way up onto the dock and her waiting towel. Stripping off the rubber cap, she shook out her hair and toweled off. Then, sighing, she checked her watch, strapping it back on her wrist: eleven-fifteen. The late breakfast insured that she wouldn't be hungry for a while.

"Corliss!" The girl pulled herself up onto the end of the dock and held herself there with just her crossed arms. "I'm going for a walk."

"Okay, Miss Doren."

Corliss dropped back into the water, and Marla turned to survey the island. A trail, sandier than the shore, led away from the end of the dock. She ducked into the bathhouse and put on her tennis shoes, glad that Corliss had recommended them, then started up the trail.

She was quickly in thick underbrush; then the trail split, starting to curve around both sides of the hill before her, forest crowding down from the hill. Marla tossed her finger from one to the other, then went left. Two minutes later she had to choose again, this time deep beneath the trees, and to be contrary she chose to go to the right.

Five minutes later she regretted her decision. The trail had suddenly petered out into a jumbled pile of rocks. She was almost to the gash between the two hills; the way ahead looked easier. From here she could see the trail on the other side of the island. It seemed broader, easier than the one she had taken to get here. The way across the gap was rugged, but it was no worse than turning back.

She pushed on, crossing a sharp-angled slope slippery with dried pine needles; in places it was necessary to hold on to the trees while she leaped across sharper slopes. Ahead was a fallen tree, broken by lightning, the break charred with ashes from the resultant fire. The downed tree blocked the easy way; the only choice was to go up, around it, or down to the bottom of the slope.

Marla didn't like the look of the rocks below. She decided to go up, grabbing a sapling for support. She was almost to her goal when one foot shot out from beneath her, and then the other.

"Oh!"

Startled, she grabbed for another sapling as she started to slide—and missed. She scrabbled for a hold, without success, her body picking up speed. She slammed into another sapling, its thin trunk breaking and scourging her flailing arm.

"Oh, no! Help!"

Desperation made her grab for another sapling as she sped by; her shoulder joints wrenched, but she held on for dear life, while the sapling's roots pulled free, spilling a shower of needles. Marla began to slide again, but she had changed direction. A thicker tree was just ahead; grab that, and she'd be all right—

The tree was coming fast. She threw herself over onto her stomach, reaching with all her strength, forcing her eyes to stay open even though her vision was blurred with perspiration. There! Another two yards and she'd have it—

The ground opened beneath her and Marla fell into instant blackness. . . .

Eleven

Marla heard voices, faint and jumbled; at least one of them was shouting. It was comfortable here. Why didn't they shut up and leave her in peace? Let her sleep . . .

Sharp pains penetrated the haze over her consciousness: something digging into her hip. That was the worst, but there were other pains, and duller aches underlying each of them. She started to raise her head, and winced; the whole back of her skull was a single bruise.

Marla opened her eyes and stared up at the sky, which was as cloudless as ever; but that stupid tree leaned across her line of sight, blocking most of her view. If it would get out of the way, the sun could touch her, soak its warmth into her chilled bones. She should have changed out of her wet bathing suit before tramping off into lord-knows-where!

"This way, Jack! She's up here!"

That was Skelly; his piping voice penetrated the slot in the rocks where she lay, and made her head ache again. For heaven's sake, Skelly, shut up!

Something ran across her arm. Marla's nose wrinkled as she caught the odor of decaying leaf mold. She closed her eyes again. Maybe they'd all go away. All she wanted to do was rest here in the ground where she had fallen. Was that too much to ask?

"Marla?" That was Jack Franklin. Conceited puppy! She opened her eyes in time to see Jack turn away and call to the others, "Here she is!"

"Is she all right?" Garman was beside him, breathing heavily, bending, his hands on his thighs. His jacket was gone, but his vest was still impeccably buttoned. Why was his tie jerked loose from his collar? That would never do, Mr. Gibson! Remember the proprieties!

"I don't know," said Jack, anxious. He dropped to his knees, peering into the slot at the girl ten feet below. "Marla! Can you hear me?"

"Ohhhhh!" She tried to shift position. "Ow!"

"She's alive!"

There were others around the lip of the slot now: Philippe, Steiner, Helmer, and a scowling man wearing work clothes.

"Take it easy!" called Jack. "I'm coming down to you, Marla! Somebody hook the rope around that tree."

He tested the hitch around his waist, then sat down on the edge of the slot, small stones and dirt and a shower of dry needles falling on the girl below. Marla closed her mouth, then opened it and spat. Ugh! Why did everything hurt so?

Jack swung into the opening and maneuvered carefully, for there was little space to spare around the fallen girl. The slot opened onto the side of the hill, but the gap through the two big rocks that were responsible for the hole was only a few inches wide. He touched ground, pulled

180

enough rope to give himself freedom to move, and bent to examine Marla.

"How do you feel?"

"Terrible . . . Ow! Take it easy!"

His fingers moved away from her arm, touched other parts of her body, then moved to lift her skull, probing at the massive bruise there as Marla winced again.

"How is she?" demanded Garman. "Any broken bones?"

"I don't think so. Maybe a concussion—there's a nasty bruise on the back of her head. Yeah, she hit a rock." He scooped the offending fragment out of the leaf mold and tossed it aside. "That seems the worst of it."

The children were crowding around the slot now, peering down. They seemed so serious! Everyone seemed so serious. Hadn't they ever seen somebody fall into a stupid hole before?

"Can you stand?"

"I don't know. I'll try."

Jack's hands caught her shoulders and then her head as she sat up, gasping with pain again. Her eyes shut tight and she sucked in sudden breath, leaning against him as he probed the bruise on the back of her skull again. God, her hair must be a mess! How would she ever get it clean?

"Easy, Marla! That's right, hold on to me."

Somehow she was on her feet, swaying, held up only by his strong arms. Jack was strong; she smelled his sweat as she leaned against him, and beneath it the greasier odor of his hair tonic. Marla's cheek rested against the ridge of his collar bone, and she was aware of the swell of pectoral muscles pressing tightly against her body.

181

The rope went around her body, snug beneath her arms, bristly bits of hemp digging into her soft skin until an itch began. Jack tested the loop by lifting on it.

"Okay! Take her up—easy!"

Marla's head hung, eyes still closed, as the others pulled her from the slope; Jack held her hands against her sides as though afraid that the rope would slip over her arms. Then she sat on the edge, the rope coming loose, hands lifting her and laying her on something taut. It was much better than the ground. Wool covered her to her neck and was tucked in around her body.

"Okay, easy now, fellows."

That was Garman. As the litter was lifted into the air, Marla opened her eyes in time to see Jack come out of the hole, pulling himself hand over hand up the rope. He dusted himself off.

"You got her okay?" he asked, anxious.

"We have her," came the guttural reply. Marla rolled her eyes up and saw Steiner and Helmer at the corners of the litter. Then she rolled them down, recognized Philippe's back, although he wore only an undershirt and his striped trousers. The stranger in work clothes was on the other pole; he must be Cassini, the stablemaster.

"Easy!" cried Garman as the litter jerked.

"Ohhhhh!" Marla cried in pain, then slipped back into blessed unconsciousness. The litter jerked repeatedly as the men made their way across the slope to the trail, then picked a careful way back to the cove. But she knew none of it. It was not until the speedboat moved out onto the lake and spray hit her face that she came awake and realized that the litter was across the prow of the boat.

Jack was at the wheel; the four litter bearers and Garman crouched in the cockpit, Steiner and Cassini where they could keep one balancing hand on the end poles of the litter.

"I don't feel so good," said Marla.

"Small wonder," said Garman. "Take it easy, Miss Doren—we'll have you back at the house in a few minutes."

Her eyes closed again, until the motor changed pitch and Jack nudged the boat against the dock. He held it there while Steiner and Helmer clambered up the ladder, then leaned down to take the litter from Philippe and Cassini. A moment later another motor sputtered still, a smaller boat banging against a piling as Skelly snubbed it in place and Corliss lifted the outboard out of the water. Then the children scrambled up onto the dock while the men picked up Marla.

"Is the doctor coming?" she asked.

"Soon," said Garman. "I've sent for him."

"How? Did they fix the phone?"

"Not yet. There's a telegraph key in the shelter; during the winter it's the only way Davis has to send messages. The doctor will come on the next train."

Marla was mercifully unaware of the climb into the house, nor did she hear Garman as he cursed the foolishness of his father and grandfather. As they transferred her into bed she opened her eyes long enough to ask, "What time is it?" But she was asleep before they answered.

Something ice cold touched her; Marla's eyes flew open, and she saw the doctor, listening through his stethoscope. He was white-haired, his mustache stained brown on the ends. A scowl marked his face until he saw that she was awake; then it dissolved into a smile.

"Well, young lady! How do you feel?"

"Sore," she said, closing her eyes again.

"You're very fortunate." But she didn't hear that. Nor did she wake when Mrs. Davis, with the help of Callie, stripped off her bathing suit and dressed her in her pajamas.

Twilight was just deepening the color of the sky when Marla woke again. Something was wrong. She blinked, and turned to look out the windows; she could see the island in the distance beyond the boathouse.

That wasn't right—she was in Corliss's room. In the girl's bed. Somebody sat in a cushioned wooden rocker near the window, leafing through one of Skelly's comic books. It was the other maid; Marla couldn't remember her name.

"What time is it?"

The girl jumped. "Oh! Miz Doren! You feel okay?"

"Except for the fiercest headache in the world. What time is it?" she asked again, patiently.

"I don't know—gettin' late, I guess."

"Is that my watch on the dresser?" The girl's eyes followed the instructions. "Get it for me, please. Thank you."

She couldn't focus on the tiny figures, although distant objects remained unblurred. At last she called the girl again, and asked her to read it: she puzzled it out with effort, then said, "Uh, almost ten o'clock."

So late to still be light! Marla yawned suddenly and started to stretch; the movement brought renewed achings. She moved her head gingerly.

The girl edged away, stammering, "Uh, I'm s'posed to tell them when you woke up."

"All right." Marla forced a smile. "Thank you."

"You're welcome." She bobbed her head, almost curtsied, and fled.

Marla turned back to look out the window again. The memory of what had happened was clear now. She completed an inventory of aches before the door opened and Garman came into the room.

"Are you feeling better, Miss Doren?"

"Hardly." She grimaced. "I'm sorry, Mr. Gibson—I made a fool of myself."

"You certainly did," he agreed. "Whatever impulsed you to go crawling around those rocks."

"The only honest answer is stupidity. If Skelly or Corliss had tried it I'd have called them away." Then she added anxiously, "If I still had a job."

"Certainly you have a job. I will admit I didn't expect you to demonstrate the wrong way to do something first. The doctor says there's no permanent damage, although you'll have that headache for a while. Tomorrow you're to stay in bed. You can get up Saturday if you behave yourself."

"I'll behave myself."

"I'm sure you will," said Garman, dryly. "Are you hungry?"

She never did get the picnic lunch—the second

185

day in a row she had missed out on two meals. Marla hoped it wasn't going to prove a habit.

"Yes."

"Mrs. Davis is heating some soup. I'll have her send up a tray."

"Thank you." She glanced around the room, the shadows deepening. "I'm sorry to have pushed Corliss out of her bed."

"Nonsense; Corliss thinks this is an adventure. She's delighted to have the chance to sleep in Skelly's room. Saturday we'll move you back to your own room, if you're up to it—perhaps we should find you something on this level."

"I'm sure I'll be all right by Saturday," Marla said quickly. "I don't want you to have any further problems because of me."

"It's no problem, Miss Doren. Rooms are something we have in quantity. I think there's an empty one between Tim and Philippe; yes, I'm sure of it. It's not as private as your present room, but it will save you some climbing, at least until you've fully recovered."

"Thank you," she said again.

Garman stood. "Do you want someone to stay with you tonight—help you to the bath? Mrs. Davis can send one of the girls."

"I don't think so." Marla tested her strength, sat up on the edge of the bed, then pulled herself to her feet, wincing. "No. It hurts, but I can walk. If you don't mind, though—would you hand me my slippers and robe?"

"Certainly."

She sat down again to put on her slippers, and winced again as she pulled the robe over her arms. It seemed as though every muscle in her body had a separate ache. Being upright made her head ache more furiously.

"One more favor, if you don't mind, Mr. Gibson—the lamp?"

He smiled, pumping up the gas lamp on the nightstand and lighting it; the harsh glare banished the shadows around that side of the bed.

"I'll light the lamp in the bath too—one of the kerosene lamps; it will burn all night without attention."

After making certain that Marla could navigate without help, he preceded her to the end of the hall. The bathroom seemed smaller than the bath upstairs, but the fixtures were new; the tub had a shower, which drew Marla's envious attention. But that was more than she could manage tonight.

"Is there anything else?" Garman asked before withdrawing.

"Has Tim returned?"

"Yes." Garman smiled. "A number of people have been chomping at the bit, but I told them to leave you alone. I'll send him up."

Then he was gone, and Marla made use of the facilities, splashing water on her face to cool it when she finished. She touched the back of her head, the pain shooting across the great bruise, and tried to turn far enough to see it. But the maneuver was too much for her.

Marla had just arranged herself back in bed when a knock came at the door; she called for the person to enter, and Tim came in, bearing a tray.

"Well! You've had quite a day, young lady. I guess I can't leave you alone for a minute."

She forced a smile. "And what about your day? Did you buy the local telephone company?"

"It wasn't necessary—the Gibsons already own a third of the stock. All I had to do was remind the line boss that Garman was ready to tell his draft board that his job was no longer essential. They finished about an hour ago. This time I think the line will stay together awhile."

The tray had folding legs. Tim helped Marla arrange the pillows so that she could sit up, then arranged the tray over her lap. She removed the cover from the bowl and was almost overwhelmed by the rich smell of the meaty soup.

"Mmmm! Heavenly!"

There were thick slices of hot bread in a napkin-covered basket, and a little crock of sweet butter. Warmth spread pleasantly through Marla's middle as she sipped at the soup. Tim drew a chair to the side of the bed and sat down, his hands clasped between his legs, leaning forward a bit, watching her.

"Marla . . ."

She swallowed a bite of bread and sipped at the glass of water. "Please, Tim. Not now."

"Now," he said stubbornly. "This morning I said there were things I should have told you four years ago. It hasn't taken me this long to realize my mistake, Marla—I knew it six months after I left Lyons Falls. I should have come back then."

"Why didn't you?" she asked gently.

He shrugged. "Stubborn pride—fear that you would reject me, laugh at me. God knows you had every right to laugh at me after I walked out on you that way. Marla, I'm trying to say I'm sorry!

I want us to back up four years, start over again. This time we can make it."

"Are you asking me to marry you?"

He hesitated. "Well . . . yes! Dammit, yes! I want you to marry me, Marla. I want to marry you. Will you?"

Her appetite was gone. Marla lay back, sighing. "Take the tray, please."

Tim pulled the burden away and helped her settle down into the pillows. Then he sat again, edging closer, taking her hand in his.

"Marry me, Marla. Please!"

"I . . . don't know. I was going to say I can't, Tim, but I just don't know. Four years is a long time—we've both changed. I know I have. How do I know we can call back what we used to feel for each other?"

"When will you know?" he demanded.

"We have all summer. I want to get to know you again, Tim, find out just how you have changed. I know you'll be coming and going, but we'll have time. Plenty of time."

"Not as much as you think," he said roughly. But when she pressed for an explanation, he said only, "All right. I'll do it your way. I don't like it, but I owe you that much, Marla. I owe you everything. I do love you."

"I once thought I loved you. . . ."

"You will again!"

Marla sighed. "Please, I want to change the subject. Tell me, who is Andrew?"

"Andrew who?"

Marla studied him closely. "The name means nothing to you—has no connection with Beechhaven?"

189

"Not unless it's Cassini—no; his name is Enzio. I saw it once on the payroll. Why?"

Marla wanted to share her burden; then she remembered Corliss's fright, and wondered if she had any right to widen the child's circle of fear.

"I thought I heard the name," she said. "Tell me about Garman's brothers."

"His brother, you mean. There's only the one—George. He was in Europe when the Nazis overran France, and he sent Philippe to England with most of the branch's assets. He stayed behind to try and pick up the pieces—too long, the way it turned out. After Pearl Harbor, the Nazis interned him in Germany."

"Do you know him?"

"I've met him, yes. More often than I'd like. Betwixt thee, me, and the bedpost, George is a slippery character. I would never trust him."

"What about Garman? What do you think of him?"

The question was the one she had asked yesterday, the answer carefully avoided. For a moment she thought his reaction was going to be the same. Then Tim twisted his mouth.

"Garman is . . . intelligent."

"But ruled by his mother?"

"There is that, yes, although I'm sure Alicia has less control of Garman than she thinks. He gives in to her in matters he considers of little or no concern."

"What does concern him?"

"Gibson Industries International."

"And that's all? Nothing else?"

"Anything else comes a distant second. Garman has a computer for a heart, Marla. I don't think

190

he's capable of love, not in the way you and I . . . the way I love you. He takes care of his possessions because he has an investment to protect. He takes care of his family because they represent a certain status in the eyes of the world. That's why he made Bethel come here this year, and why she took to her bed."

"And the children?"

"The kids don't disobey, as Bethel tried to do. If their father lays down the law, then that's it. Basically they're pretty good kids, but Bethel spoils them and Garman ignores them."

"Leaving Alicia the strongest force in their lives."

"Leaving Alicia to dominate them as she dominated her own children, and still tries to do when she exercises her control over Garman."

Marla's heart went out to the children; she glanced toward the wall, as though she could see them in the beds two rooms over. She thought of her own father. The poor kids, given substitutes for love by three people incapable of knowing what love should be!

"Tell me about Garman's older brother, Gabriel—the one who died."

"Oh. Chris—that happened twenty-five years ago. Although Alicia still dotes on his memory. I'm told her bedroom is practically a museum. She still has all his toys and clothes up there—packs them up and takes them along every time the family changes houses."

"But what happened?"

"As I understand, a swimming accident—Alicia and the other two boys were the only witnesses. Apparently the three of them were playing around the diving raft—not the one there now: Alicia and Goulding had the other one broken up and burned. Anyway, story is that young Gabriel hit his head, whether on the raft or the diving board I couldn't say. It knocked him out, and he drowned."

"But his brothers were there—why didn't they help him?"

Tim shrugged. "I guess there was nothing they could do. He went under, then came up under the raft. By the time the divers found his body it was too late. I do know that Corliss and Skelly practically had to beg before Alicia consented to the new raft."

Marla shuddered. "And his mother saw everything—how terrible! From the tower, I suppose."

"No. The accident happened just before the First World War. Goulding had the tower built right after the war ended, but I think Alicia designed it herself. When she's alone she spends most of her time, day and night, sitting and looking out at the lake."

Until this moment Marla had not thought it possible that she could feel pity for Alicia Gibson; but the empathy was there. She could imagine herself in Alicia's place. What a terrible waste of a life, waiting only for the moments that could be spent staring into yesterday!

She sighed. "I'm tired, Tim. We'll talk again ... about everything."

He took her hand. "I do love you, Marla."

That might be enough. . . .

When Marla didn't answer, Tim bent over her and pressed his lips to her forehead, then to her lips. Marla accepted the kiss passively, forcing herself not to respond. Oh, God! She closed her eyes. Did she still love him? Was it too late to love him?

Thinking that she was asleep, he stood over her a moment longer, then moved quietly from the room; Marla heard the floorboards shift beneath his weight and the tiny sound when the latch clicked home. Her eyes opened again and she looked after him. But all that met her eyes was a large rag doll, smiling vacantly from a chair, in everlasting sympathy.

Her eyes closed again but sleep was far away; Marla felt as though she would never need sleep again. She cataloged the aches in her body again, probing at a tooth that seemed loose until pain stabbed; after that she left it alone, and turned her attention to the house.

All around her it creaked, signs that the house was alive, indications that people below or above were moving about. The cry of a nightbird came through the window, answered by the hoot of an owl and the rush of wings; a moment later came the scream of a cat in the woods. A wildcat, she decided; she'd seen no pets about the house. Perhaps Alicia disapproved.

Someone coughed on the porch below: Philippe, sneaking another smoke? And someone was moving in the hall outside; footsteps approached the door lightly, but they were caught by Marla's suddenly hypersensitive hearing. The knob turned, the door opened, and Corliss peeked in.

"Miss Doren?" It was a whisper, in case Marla was asleep.

"I'm here, Corliss. Come in."

The girl approached, seeming even younger in

short-legged seersucker pajamas; a doll was tucked under her arm.

"Do you feel better?"

"A little," said Marla. She smiled. "At least I'm alive. How did you ever find me in that hole?"

"Skelly found you."

"A remarkable job. I could have lain there for days."

"Andrew showed him where you were."

Corliss sat in the chair abandoned by Tim, in almost the same position, except for the doll dangling between her legs. She sighed, chest rising and falling once, then met Marla's eyes.

"Don't you want to ask me about him?"

Corliss's expression was free of guile, and there was no trace of the terrifying fear. The change was astonishing.

Marla chose her words with care. "I thought we couldn't mention his name."

"That was before. We talked it over, the three of us, and I convinced Skelly you were on our side. I can tell that about people—I'm never wrong. I made Andrew listen, but it was his idea to tell you now. He says you can help us, Marla."

The slip back into familiarity was caught, but, studying the girl, Marla decided not to make an issue of it. She knew Corliss was begging her to be friends . . . and there was only one way she could respond.

"Help you how?"

Corliss tossed her head, but it was plain that Marla had passed the first part of the test. "I can't tell you yet. You got to ask the other questions first."

194

Marla sat up, wincing, and folded her hands in her lap. The effort was costly, but she felt at a disadvantage lying down.

"You won't explain unless I play the game?"

A quick shake of the head. "I can't. But it's not a game. I'm not playing."

"All right, I'll try to guess his identity."

"You won't, but you can try."

The effort of sitting was too much; Marla dropped flat again, wincing as her head touched the pillow. Then she sighed, closing her eyes.

"I'm sorry, Corliss. I'm really not up to guessing games. Please, tell me who he is."

"Our uncle."

Eyes open, Marla turned her head. "Your mother's brother?"

"Uh-uh." Another quick shake of the head. "Mother doesn't have any brothers or sisters."

"Then you mean your Uncle George. But I thought he was a prisoner of war, in Germany."

"He's not. Not in Germany, I mean. He's right here, hiding in Grandfather Goulding's room. He's why Liz thinks I've been stealing food, but I haven't. But it isn't him, either."

Marla tried to follow the convoluted rush of statements, then gave up. Corliss had tensed, edging forward on her seat, knees clamped about the doll.

"You mean George isn't Andrew. Andrew isn't George."

"No, they're not—he's not."

"But . . . Corliss, George Gibson is your only uncle! Unless your mother or father was married before."

"They weren't." Corliss was jiggling now. "It's not a trick, Marla—not this time."

Marla gave up; her head was throbbing again. "There's no one left, Corliss."

Another minute passed, Corliss studying her without saying a word. Then the girl got up and went to her dresser, looking around quickly to see if Marla was watching as she rummaged beneath an untidy stack of clothes in the bottom drawer. She came back with a framed photograph and pressed it into Marla's hand.

Marla studied Corliss a few seconds longer as the girl dropped back into the chair, leaning back this time, hands dangling and doll dragging on the floor. Her pigtails were hidden; in that position she looked more than ever like a boy.

Marla looked at the photograph and recognized the boy instantly. It was a studio portrait, posed even though his smile was as broad as in the picture down on the gallery wall.

It was the boy in the group photo, although this had been taken a year or two earlier. He was alone, dressed in knickers and plaid knee socks that were unnaturally straight, wearing a four-in-hand knot in his tie that managed to look crooked even when perfect. Except for a cowlick, his hair was slicked down.

Marla studied the photo for a moment, comparing it with her memory of the other. Then she looked at Corliss.

"This is Gabriel."

Corliss nodded, swinging the doll again. "Gabriel was his first name. He hated it when he was alive 'cause he hated his grandfather."

When he was alive . . .

.Marla swallowed. "Corliss ..."

Corliss answered the unasked question: "Now he uses his middle name—Gabriel Andrew Gibson."

Twelve

Marla's mouth hung open, a single laugh chopped off as she read the look in the girl's eye. Corliss stared back, tensed, her eyes blazing defiance; the doll slipped from her fingers to lie with head at crooked angle against the floor. Marla swallowed, then remembered to close her mouth.

"Andrew is . . ." She couldn't say it.

"Dead," finished Corliss, with a shrug.

He was a ghost. A ghost . . .

With the revelation, Marla again wanted to laugh, but turned it into a sigh. Her eyes closed for a moment, her fingertips resting on the glass frame of the photograph. It seemed hot to her touch and she yanked her hand away.

In the silence, the night sounds of the house came back, louder than before: an incessant background symphony of life, belying the view of city people who thought that the country was as quiet as the grave. . . . No! Wrong image, Marla! Then she heard Corliss breathing, air hissing in and out in quick, anxious suckings.

She opened her eyes and stared for a moment at the canopy overhead before turning to meet the child's bright eyes.

"Where is Andrew now?"

Corliss shrugged. "I don't know."

"He isn't here, in this room?"

"If he was, I'd know it. You'd probably know it too—at least, if he wanted you to."

"I'd see him?"

"No."

"Do you see Andrew?"

"Sometimes."

"Only some of the time?"

"Sometimes he can't let us see him."

Marla sighed again, relaxing. "Whenever grownups are around?"

"No!" Corliss sat up and leaned forward to grab the edge of the mattress, bunching the fabric of the sheet that was Marla's only cover. Marla glanced down and saw the girl's knuckles turn white.

"Grownups can't ever see him, Marla—only Skelly and I can see him, and that's only because we're blood relatives and we've been coming here ever since we were born."

"Then even if Andrew were to come here right now, into this room, I couldn't see him."

"No. If he wanted you to know he was here, you would feel him."

Watching eyes . . .

Malevolent eyes!

Marla shuddered, thinking that she was smothering a laugh. Her eyes darted about the room, touching each corner, each dark shadow, despite Corliss's assurances that Andrew—the ghost!—was not present at the moment.

"Did . . ."

Marla's voice cracked. What was the matter with her? She didn't believe this mad story! She

199

couldn't believe such nonsense! She was a rational, sensible adult....

She wet her dry lips and started again. "Did ... Andrew ... come to my room, Corliss? Yesterday?"

The girl sat back in the chair, relaxing; she knew that Marla had accepted the story.

She nodded. "When you first came. He says now he's sorry he scared you. He thought you were gonna be like Miss Hurst, watching us every minute. He figured if he could frighten you away from here, Father might give up, not try to get somebody else to take your place until we went back to New York."

"Does Andrew go to New York with you?"

"No. He can't leave here, not until ... That's why we need your help, Marla."

The watching eyes had not been her imagination....

But they had been malevolent.

Marla shuddered at the memory, as fear rose again, unbidden, in automatic response to the unknown and the unknowable. She felt a sudden chill and rubbed her arms. Ghosts were supposed to take heat from a room—was Andrew here now? Watching her?

She asked, but Corliss shook her head. "I haven't seen him in over an hour. I think maybe he's keeping an eye on Uncle George, or on those men who came last night. There was supposed to be another one, but something happened to him—Andrew says the other ones are mad at Father, blame him for it."

That explained Garman's reactions this morning, perhaps Philippe's as well. If not for the more pressing problem of Andrew, Marla's curiosity would have demanded to know why Steiner and Helmer were here.

She shrugged away the thought, returning her attention to Corliss. The child seemed sincere, but might this not be only another elaborate joke? Practical joking ran in the family bloodline—Tim had said that.

"Corliss, yesterday I overheard you . . . you were in the attic. Arguing with someone."

The child was instantly tense, knuckles tightening as nails dug into her palms; but her expression remained neutral. Marla hurried to explain:

"I wasn't spying—it was an accident, when I came up from your grandmother's apartment. The two of you must have been standing right over me. I could hear clearly every word you said—your words. His . . . the other person's . . . were only a mumble."

Corliss showed excitement. "You *heard* him?"

"I heard a mumble," Marla reiterated. "It did sound like a boy. You called him Andrew."

"But . . ." Corliss was almost bouncing now, no longer able to contain herself. "Marla, you're the first person besides me and Skelly to even hear him! Most people just get cold shivers up and down their spine when he's around, the way you do when you think somebody's watching you but you don't dare turn around. Maybe Andrew was right—maybe you can help us!"

"Help in what way, Corliss?"

"Help us find his murderer!"

Corliss leaned forward again as the dramatic statement once more brought silence to Marla.

Tim's description of the accident, not half an hour ago, played against the memory screen at the back of her mind. The accident, as Tim had called it . . .

Now, although the event had taken place more than ten years before her own birth, Corliss was claiming that Andrew's death had not been accidental.

"Corliss . . . at the time Andrew died, only your father and your uncle—his brothers—were with him."

Corliss nodded vehemently. "One of them did it."

"That's a terrible thing to say—to think!"

"But it's true. Andrew doesn't know which one, Marla—that's why we need your help. You're an adult, you can find out things we can't. People think we're just kids—they'll listen to you, believe you."

Not if she told madness! Aloud: "You give me credit I may not deserve, Corliss. But—your grandmother saw the accident. She saw it happen."

"She saw it happen, but it was no accident! She's lying when she says it was. Grandmother knows the truth, she's the only one besides us, but she won't tell. That's why Andrew won't go near her now. He was her favorite when he was alive, but she's protecting the murderer. She'll never tell the truth."

"His *brothers*, Corliss! They were children!"

"You think kids can't hate bad enough to kill, Marla? They hated him, both of them." The statement was flat, and therefore all the more horrible. "They hated him because he was

202

Grandmother's favorite. Parents shouldn't play favorites—I won't, if I ever have children—but they do. Some of them. Some parents are like Father—he doesn't care about either one of us."

A computer for a heart . . .

"I'm sure you're wrong, Corliss. I'm sure your father loves you, both of you."

Another quick shake of the head: the mouth set tight, Corliss's eyes burning more brightly.

"Father doesn't love anybody—he never loved anybody, not even Mother. He ignores us, Marla, except when we make too much noise or something. Then he chases us away. Skelly hates him—I think some part of Father is missing, was never there like it is in normal people, so I just feel sorry for him. But Skelly hates him so much it sometimes makes him sick."

The currents of hatred in this house ran deeper than Marla could have imagined. Now that the words were out, Corliss seemed drained as she slumped in her chair. Marla could see perspiration streaking the child's neck and legs, although with darkness the breeze coming straight off the lake had cooled the house and filled the room with the scent of forest growth. She breathed deeply through her nose, savoring the pine; then she again caught the harsher odor of smoke.

Marla wet her lips again, just to have something to do, something that would delay speaking a moment longer. How much of Corliss's mad story was true? How much only fancy on the part of the children? Her resentment, and probably Skelly's too, must color the facts. How could a parent, a father, feel *nothing* for his own flesh?

203

Oh, marriages could fail; but a parent must have some special feeling for his children!

A soft rapping sounded at the door, barely heard; Corliss came out of her chair, tensed, nostrils flaring and eyes wide in sudden fear. She stared at the door, then darted a quick glance at Marla.

The door opened just far enough for Skelly to peer in. He whispered, "Corliss? Is everything all right?"

Corliss sighed, then laughed, collapsing into the chair again. "Everything's fine, Skelly. You can come in." Then she looked at Marla. "It's okay, isn't it, if he comes in?"

Marla shrugged, and Skelly slipped through the door. He wore pajamas like his sister's, although his were imprinted with sports figures in virile action, while Corliss's were sprinkled with appealingly unreal kittens and puppies. He came to stand behind the chair, eyes large as he stared at Marla.

"Is she going to help us?" he asked softly.

"Yes!"

"If I can," said Marla. "To be honest, Corliss, I'm not sure what you expect me to do. I can't force a confession from . . . your father, or your uncle. Nor do I see a way to make your grandmother tell the truth, if she's been lying for twenty-five years."

She forced a small laugh. "I'm not a detective, not like Charlie Chan or Philo Vance or Sam Spade. I don't even read detective stories. I'm not sure even a real detective would know where to start, trying to solve a murder that happened twenty-five years ago."

"Tim's a detective," said Skelly.

"What?" Marla had thought she was beyond astonishment.

"That's what Andrew says," said the boy.

"No, that isn't at all what Andrew said, Skelly!" His sister shook her head as though disgusted. "He said Tim acts like a detective, or a policeman, the way he tries to find out what Father's doing."

How much could one mind take? Was nothing in the world what it seemed to be? Marla shook her head, trying to remember back to when life seemed sane—God only two days ago! Troubled, yes; but sane.

Now everything was madness!

Still, if Tim was something more than he claimed to be, as Andrew (if *he* was real, and not a figment of the children's imagination!) suspected . . . Marla shook her head again, losing control of her thoughts. If Tim was a detective or a policeman, maybe he could help.

The curtains whipped in sudden breeze, the temperature of the room dipping sharply; the lamp flickered, its glow fading from white to a softer yellow. Marla felt a sudden chill against her spine; as Corliss had said, it was as though someone was watching her. This time, however, there was an absence of malevolence.

"Is . . . Andrew here now?"

Corliss nodded. "Yes. He just came."

"You see him?"

"No," said Skelly. "He hasn't got enough energy—he had to use it up when Corliss called him to the island to find you."

"He's tied here," said Corliss. "To the lake,

where it happened, and to the house, because his body was here while his spirit finished breaking away. It hurt him bad to go to the island."

"He has to stay here," said Skelly. "He can't leave."

"Not ever?" asked Marla.

"Not while the person who hated him so much he had to kill him is still free," said the boy.

"And if the guilty one is never found out, never punished?"

There was a moment of silence while the children's eyes drifted out of focus and they listened; Marla strained to hear with them, but there was nothing—nothing aural—but the feeling of a fourth presence was undiminished.

Corliss broke first, her face sober. She blinked, and rubbed the back of her hand across her mouth.

"We have to find the guilty one, Marla. Otherwise Andrew will have to stay here for—well, not forever. But for a long long time."

"Until his spirit dies," said Skelly.

The lamp flared bright again, the temperature soaring back to normal; the weight of the unseen presence was gone as though it had never been. Marla blinked and looked at the children again.

"He's gone," said Corliss. "He just wanted to be sure you were going to help."

It was then that Marla realized she had made her decision. Fantasy or not, the children believed in Andrew. It was her place to do whatever she could to help them, even if they were touched with madness.

"If I can," she said. "*If* I can."

"You can do it," said Corliss, assured. "Andrew says you can, Marla."

Skelly yawned widely, and Marla glanced at her watch; there was no problem reading it now: past eleven.

"You two better get to bed before somebody finds out you're up."

"Oh, nobody comes up here, except the girls when they have to clean or something. And that's only during the day." Skelly yawned again while his sister talked. "Even Tim and Jack won't come up here."

"I thought you played games with them," said Marla.

"Only in the parlor. Mother doesn't like them to come to this part of the house." Corliss thought for a minute, then added, "She doesn't like them, period."

"She doesn't trust them," said Skelly.

"That's because they were hired by Father," said Corliss. "Mother thinks he set them to spy on her."

"She's wrong," said Skelly. "Liz is the spy. She tells Father everything. I tried to tell Mother that Liz was just sucking up to her, pretending she was her friend, but Mother wouldn't listen."

The news was another surprise, but not a shock: Marla had known instinctively, when she first saw the woman this morning, that Liz Davis was a troubled soul. Confirmation that she carried a grudge against the world made her feel sorry for Davis. And for the girls under her thumb. Alicia and Bethel might be as demanding as Tim had said, but Liz Davis ran the house and made their life hell.

"What about Mr. Davis?"

"Oh, Davis is okay," said Corliss, shrugging. "I feel sorry for him, married to Liz."

"Davis likes us," said Skelly. "He's good to us, 'cause he never had kids of his own."

"He's better off without them," said Corliss. "Just think of having Liz for a mother!"

"Going back to mothers," said Marla, "if the noise level doesn't go down now, she'll come out to see what you two are doing."

Corliss laughed. "Never. Mother won't open her door herself, much less come out, until Davis tells her the buggy is ready to take her out to the private car. And she won't even go then if anybody but Skelly and me is on the train."

The poor woman! Forced by an unfeeling husband to stay in a place she disliked with all her heart, forced to share this house with a woman who was her enemy! Marla could feel pity even without meeting her. She wondered what kept Bethel in such a loveless marriage. Why hadn't she walked out on Garman years ago?

The children? Marla could imagine Garman threatening to take Corliss and Skelly away from their mother, refusing her the right even to see them. How could she ever have thought him attractive? She remembered Tim's description of George as a thoroughly unlikable character; but Garman was no better, perhaps worse.

Two bad pennies: which one was a childhood murderer?

Skelly yawned again. "Bed!" said Marla. "Now—move, the two of you. We'll talk more tomorrow. The doctor said I have to stay in bed until Saturday, so I won't be able to do anything before then."

Corliss shrugged. "That's okay. Nothing's going to happen before then."

"Before we go, do you need anything?" asked Skelly, his voice soft; his solicitous kindness surprised Marla. "A drink of water?"

Marla considered. "Water, yes. Thank you, Skelly."

When he returned, Corliss helped fluff the pillows so that she could sit up, and asked if Marla wanted something to read. But her thoughts were too full; she would never be able to concentrate on the mundane world of popular entertainment.

"No. I want to think. You two have given me a lot to think about. Turn the lamp down before you go, please. Yes, that's far enough, Corliss."

The children said good-night and left. Marla sipped at the water, staring at nothing, then lowered the glass to her lap, hands folded around it, thumbs rubbing against the cut design. It was amazing that the water could be so cold in such hot weather. The supply must come from a deep well, perhaps a spring.

The moon was up high enough to color the lake. Marla stared out the window and saw the line of pines on the island, only slighter blacker than the starry sky. The breeze stirred the curtains; she could hear the night life again, a cricket chirping, a tree frog calling. She remembered the cricket in her room, and wondered how it had come to be so high in the house. She wiggled her toes against the sheet, moved her legs back and forth, and watched the motion.

She sighed; Marla knew she was ignoring the

question. Murder . . . no matter how it was said, it was something out of another world. There had been no deaths by violence in Lyons Falls, nor in any of the surrounding villages, within her memory. Crime was something you read about in the newspapers; it happened in New York or Chicago, or maybe came as close as Utica or Syracuse, but it never happened in your own hometown. People in Lyons Falls didn't have to lock their doors for fear of thieves or murderers!

She sighed again—lately all she was doing was sighing!—and reached to put the glass on the nightstand, stretching half a dozen aches back into activity. Wincing, Marla sat back, squirming against the pillows and shifting until she felt satisfied. The breeze seemed stronger, the smell of smoke heavier in the night air. How close was the fire? Could Beechhaven be in any danger?

Tim Layard . . . a policeman!

Marla laughed at the thought, preposterous on the face of it. People like Tim weren't policemen—the image of Pat O'Brien popped into her mind: he was a policeman, just as Humphrey Bogart was Sam Spade and Ralph Bellamy was Ellery Queen. Who played Perry Mason? She couldn't remember. Basil Rathbone, of course, was Sherlock Holmes. Watson, the game's afoot! If only fiction were real!

It *was* a game—something to be played. Now that the children were no longer here to convince her, by their own strong belief, Marla found it impossible to accept the ghost of a dead boy. Andrew, you're a figment!

Yet, the sensation of his presence . . . She shivered. If Gabriel Andrew Gibson had been murdered, robbed of life in his childhood, then his murderer deserved punishment, no matter who he was. In the movies the murderer always was punished, the detective always got his man.

The children, Andrew included, credited her with more than she was capable of achieving. Help—before Marla could help them, she needed it herself. If not Tim, who?

Philippe? Like Alicia, he was pathetic, holding to a past irrevocably gone. His world had crashed in flames, could never come back. How could he help someone else when he himself needed the crutch of outlandish costume to convince himself that the past was not dead?

Jack Franklin? Jack was young, strong, adventurous enough to approach a girl in the hopes of stirring response; but he was too impetuous, let his emotions run before his brains. Tell him there was a murderer in the house and he would go off whooping in all directions. . . .

George Gibson! In the maelstrom of other happenings, Marla had not thought to question his presence. Why was he here, and not in Germany? Why was he in hiding?

Steiner and Helmer . . . not kidnappers, but perhaps desperate men. (If any of the statements attributed to Andrew could be believed.) Angry with Garman, who was concerned over . . . what? The mere fact of their presence? His brother, in hiding?

His own guilty conscience?

No; Marla rejected that notion. If Garman was indeed capable of murder, had murdered, the burden rested lightly on any vestigial conscience he might possess. She knew there were people totally lacking in such spiritual censors; they were the ones capable of evil in its worst manifestations. If Garman was capable of feelings, he managed to conceal the fact from those who should know him best—his children.

But could an inability to love even his own flesh mark him deficient in other emotions?

Murder, a quarter of a century old . . .

A floorboard creaked in the hall and a soft knocking sounded at the door. Marla twisted around. "Who is it?"

The door opened, revealing Philippe. He slouched as he filled the narrow opening, his face longer than nature had intended in the design.

"I hope I didn't wake you, Marla."

"No. But it is very late, Philippe."

"I'm sorry—I wanted to talk to you. To somebody."

Dejection was marked in his face, and Marla took pity. "All right, then. Come in."

He closed the door carefully, easing it into the frame, and took the chair abandoned by Tim and Corliss. Philippe wore the same sweater and slacks as he had last night; he studied her for a moment, slumping in the chair, long hands on his bony knees. Then he sighed.

"What is it?" asked Marla, impatient. "You didn't come here at this time of night to gawk and sigh like a lovesick teen-ager, I hope."

"Sick, yes, Marla. Lovesick, no. There was a time I could fall in love just seeing a pretty face such as yours, but no more. There are many times I wish I were a teen-ager again. The world was so much easier then."

"Yesterday is gone, Philippe. Like it or not, we

have to live in the world today. Or would you rather be like Alicia Gibson, caught forever in yesterday?"

The shot struck home; he straightened, backbone picking up his shoulders.

"What do you know of yesterday?" he demanded.

"Everything. I was in love then. I was happy. The future was bright. It all vanished, all of it. Everyone has problems, Philippe—the world revolves on problem. Not wars, but little things, such as grief for loved ones, the knowledge that you did something wrong that you cannot undo. What did you do?"

"I left my country. My family."

"So? Would you be happier to go back now, live under the Nazis? If you really want to do something for your family, why don't you join the Free French forces? Fight for your country? Stop living in yesterday—get rid of that silly dress suit."

It poured out, all the venom and bitterness stored up since the day Tim walked out of her life. Philippe stared in horror as Marla continued to rip him apart, but she couldn't stop the vituperation, couldn't slow her words or turn them to reason.

"You know what I thought the first time I saw you, Philippe? A wedding cake. Spun-sugar dolls. You have just about that much substance—oh, God!"

She buried her face in her hands, the tears flowing freely, body shaking and bedsprings creaking. It was too much, it was all too much! Beechhaven was supposed to be a place for her to hide, to recover from everything in life that had gone wrong . . . but first Tim, then the children with their ghost . . . how was she supposed to cope? She couldn't take anymore!

"Oh, God help me! Help me!"

Philippe's hands caught Marla's shoulders, his arms going around her. She collapsed against him, burying her face against his chest, and he held her while it came out in the tears and the anger, the self-recriminations that tore apart her last defenses. He held her close, his face pressed against her hair, the aches and hurts stabbing through muscle tissue but ignored as Marla soaked his sweater until the hot tears were exhausted, until only dry sobs shook her, until there was nothing at all left inside. . . .

"Oh, God! . . . ."

He was murmuring softly, the same words over and over, as his long fingers held her tightly, his strong arms giving a circle of protection. "It's all right, Marla. Cry it out. Everything's going to be all right. . . ."

Marla blinked, vision blurry, wet eyelashes tangled. She sniffed, and again, and he dug a handkerchief from his pocket and pressed it into her fingers. She wiped her face and then her nose, and then blew, sniffing away the last of the tears when that was done.

"Thank you," she said, her voice small.

"Thank you, Marla."

She looked up, saw his serious eyes studying her, and pulled away until she could see his full face. "For what? Making a fool of myself?"

"No—for convincing me, showing me, that I have been the fool. You are right, I've lived in yesterday—lived in the way I thought my father would want. He was very conservative, Marla. A stuffed shirt. I've been a stuffed shirt. But no more."

He smiled. "The formal clothes go to the dustbins as soon as I return to my room. All formal clothes. Should it become necessary before the war ends, I will rent white tie and tails. Thank you, Marla Doren, for saying out loud what my heart has been trying to say."

The kiss took her by surprise, but it was not the kiss of last night: Philippe's lips brushed across her mouth and touched her cheek, then he released her and sat back.

"Are you all right now?"

Marla dabbed at her eyes again with his handkerchief, and managed a small laugh. "Yes. If you can say the same."

Philippe smiled. "Marla, you can't imagine how many times I've faced myself in my mirror, telling myself in the same words everything you just said. All I needed was to hear it from someone besides myself. Last night I kissed you in hopes you . . . would be like the women I knew, I used, in my former life. Until I came here, to Beechhaven, I tried to drown myself in those women, and in alcohol. I owe Alicia thanks for her prohibition of the latter. I owe you thanks for showing me that I . . . don't need the other. . . ."

He stood, suddenly seeming younger. "Marla, I would say I love you if I thought there was a chance to win you. Knowing there is not, I say it anyway, as a friend. I envy the man you do love. If he does not see it in your eyes, he is a fool!"

Then Philippe was gone, leaving Marla staring

215

at the closed door. She raised her hand to her mouth, and realized she still held his handkerchief; she brushed it across her cheek, smiling. She lay back. . . .

Tim . . .

He could have his answer—the answer he wanted. They both had made mistakes, four years ago—Marla's had been in not fighting for him. She owed Garman Gibson thanks for that much, for bringing her back into Tim's world. . . .

Garman: had he really murdered his brother? Or was it George? If the children were right, if Tim was in some fashion a policeman, he might be interested to know that George Gibson was hiding in this house. A prisoner-of-war escaping should be greeted with brass bands, banners, publicity. Something here was very wrong. . . .

If Andrew had been murdered, the crime would be punished. . . .

(Beechhaven must be a lonely place during the long months when Corliss and Skelly were away. Andrew wouldn't have to stay here while they grew up, grew old . . . until his spirit died. . . .)

Thirteen

6:00 A.M.: Marla woke to the sound of footsteps crushing the gravel of the path. The steps were slow as they approached the house, the sound diminishing as the walker turned under the porte cochere and mounted to the porch. Then the front door closed, not quite a slam but too loud to be anything other than vindictive: Liz Davis, coming to start her day.

Marla turned to where she could read her watch on the nightstand; why was it still dark outside? (It's only four o'clock real time.) The gas lamp hissed steadily, flickering, giving no more light than a twenty-five watt bulb. Even as Marla watched, the lamp began to fade, subsiding to glowing coals in the focus of the mantles.

She listened. The air seemed still, the world outside silent; the curtains hung lifeless. The smell of fire was stronger, masking any other scent from the forest. Marla lay on her side, the room warm, the sheet shrugged down to her hips, blinking as she studied the pattern of the carpet in the faint lamplight. Then she moved her head a fraction of an inch, staring out at the starless sky. . . .

7:27 A.M.: Her eyes popped open as a gentle knocking sounded at the door. The sky was the palest of blues, fading into nothingness where the trees rose from the island and the distant shore. In the absence of clouds, the smoke haze was just thickening into visibility.

The tentative knocking came again, and the door cracked open, revealing Corliss. She saw that Marla was awake, and opened it wider. The girl was rumpled from sleep, her pajama top hiked up on near hip, front gaping to reveal her bellybutton. Skelly was behind her, peering over his sister's shoulder, his hair tousled.

"Good-morning."

A yawn. "Morning."

"Do you feel betteer?"

Marla closed one eye and took inventory. "I hurt."

"Oh. Would you like to use the bathroom first?"

A headshake. "Later."

"Do you want Liz to send your breakfast?"

"Later . . ."

9:00 A.M.: Marla could feel the heat in the air before she opened her eyes. Bed was comfort, but leather-shod feet were climbing the distant stairs, growing louder as they turned into the corridor. The knock came lightly, the door opening before she could say, "Come in."

Garman stood there, impeccable as always, in gray pinstripe this morning and small-print dark blue tie. (Doesn't he own any stripes or checks or solid colors, for cripes' sake? Or ever cut himself shaving?)

"Good-morning, Miss Doren. How do you feel?"

Yawning, Marla rolled onto her back and stretched widely; then she checked the individual aches and the small stabs of pain. They were diminished but far from gone. Her neck was stiff from her sleeping position, the back of her skull still tender. She touched the bruise and winced, rolling back onto her side.

"Not ready to jump the high hurdles, but improved."

"Good." Garman smiled. "That's a gorgeous black eye."

Marla's fingers flew to her face, touching the bruised mass; how did she get that?

"The beauty contest will have to do without me this time," she said, sighing. "But the patient is ready to get up."

"Not yet; at least not for a while. Remember what the doctor said."

"I'll go stir crazy if I have to stay in bed until tomorrow."

"You may be up sooner than you'd like."

The look on Garman's face told Marla that something was seriously wrong; then she caught the smell of woodsmoke again, stronger than earlier. She looked out the window and saw eddies in the haze; there was almost no blue left in the sky.

"The fire?"

Garman nodded. "It may come this way. The phone line just went out again, but an hour ago Racquet Lake said a storm is coming from the south. It should be here by early afternoon. But it depends on the wind. Right now it's weak, and from the west, and that's in our favor. But it

219

could shift at any moment. If it goes north, behind the fire's back, we may have to evacuate."

Marla raised herself on stiff arm. "Can we do that?"

"Don't worry—there's no problem there. The railroad is cut to the north, so service is terminating at Old Forge and Thendara; but to be safe I've ordered a locomotive. Our private car is already here. We'll have plenty of time to get out, should it be necessary. We've had fire scares before, but Beechhaven has been here sixty years with nothing worse than a smoke-blackened roof."

Marla relaxed, slumping back on the bed. It was nice to be rich, to be able to pick up the phone and tell someone: "Send me a train. Never mind the cost."

Then: "But can anything be done for the house—the furnishings?"

Garman waved a hand. "Very little is irreplaceable, and that is being packed. Don't worry, Miss Doren. Tomorrow the children will be setting off their firecrackers without a worry." He turned to leave. "I'll have Mrs. Davis send a tray now."

Marla sat up as the door closed, untangling herself from the sheet. She moved gingerly until she was in her robe, although walking was definitely easier this morning. A bath would help: she debated the wisdom of a shower, and decided in favor of it.

She was back in the bedroom, using one of Corliss's hairbrushes, when Callie appeared with the tray.

"Good morning, Callie."

The girl bobbed her head as she edged into the room, more frightened than before, if that was possible. Was it the threat of the forest fire? Or just more trouble from Liz Davis?

The Davises . . . this was their home, year round. The fire threat must be even more catastrophic to them. No matter how mean Liz might be, Marla felt pity for her.

Callie refused to answer any of her questions; she grabbed last night's tray and was gone before Marla decided where she wanted to eat. The shower had refreshed her, although her pajamas seemed soiled when she put them back on. She took the tray to the bed, arranging the pillows and then herself. Breakfast finished, she leaned over the edge of the bed to put the tray on the floor, then settled down beneath the sheet, still wearing her robe, hands folded in her lap. This was silly, she couldn't sleep any . . .

11:10 A.M.: The door burst open, the noise startling Marla from a light doze. Her head jerked around as she tried to think where she was.

A breathless Corliss hung in the door, one hand on the knob, the other on the jamb. She gasped for breath.

"Marla! You gotta get up—we have to leave! The fire is coming!"

Marla blinked, swung her legs out of bed, and nearly kicked the tray. "I'm up." She fumbled for her slippers. "All right, Corliss, I'm up."

"Get dressed right away, but don't bother with anything else—just the clothes you need to wear. The wind changed. We gotta get moving!"

The child was gone, leaving Marla just above the level of sleep. She looked around and saw the sky beyond the window almost black. It was much hotter now, but a dry heat, the forest fire sucking the moisture from the air.

Where were her clothes? The things she had worn yesterday had been taken away—perhaps were still in the bathhouse on the island. Even her swimsuit was gone.

She certainly couldn't evacuate the house in her pajamas! Despite Corliss's warning, the situation couldn't have become that desperate in two short hours. Then she coughed as an eddy of smoke, whipped thin by the rising wind of the fire, was diluted through the air surging around the house, a few thousand molecules of carbon pulled through the bedroom window, a few hundred sucked into her lungs.

Marla's eyes were stinging now; she rubbed them, wincing as her hand touched the bruise above her cheekbone. Devil! She'd have to go up to her own room—all the way downstairs and around through the main entrance. Now was the time to find one of the secret panels, a shortcut—

Even as she debated her course of action Marla left the room, hurrying down the corridor toward the stairs. Then Bethel Gibson came out of her sitting room, and Marla stopped, surprised, as the woman eyed her with suspicion.

"You're the new one—Gorman, Lorgan, something like that."

"Doren, Mrs. Gibson. Marla Doren."

Bethel was carrying a jewel case and a purse, the latter so full that her fingers were stretched to the widest. Garman's wife was short, plump,

222

not at all the sort of woman Marla had pictured. Garishly dyed red hair cascaded in curls better suited to a young girl, as was the outsized bow tie at the square neckline of her chiffon tea gown. Her fingers were bejeweled, bracelets banging together on both arms.

Bethel Gibson wore makeup—too much of it. Her cheeks were rouged and her lips bright but smeared; her eyes were painted with mascara. Diamond earrings seemed vulgar against the rest of her costume.

"Why are you dressed like that?" she demanded.

"I have to get my clothes," said Marla. "They're upstairs, in Blue South. Is there a shorter way I can take, to save time?"

Bethel sniffed. "Corliss told me what happened. Silly of you. That's what comes from poking around in places you shouldn't be."

"A shortcut," Marla said again, patiently. "So I don't have to go all the way around, Mrs. Gibson."

"Of course there's a shorter way. I told Garman it was nonsense, all over the place, right in my own bedroom! Crazy old man!"

Bethel Gibson was as flighty as a nervous bird; whether it was from the commotion of the fire or was her normal state didn't matter. Marla wanted to put her hand across the woman's mouth to shut her up.

"Can you show me the way?" she begged. "Please?"

Crossly: "I said I would!"

She had said nothing of the sort, but Marla didn't contradict her. Bethel turned, Marla following her down the corridor and into Garman's

223

sitting room. His wife didn't stop, but moved quickly, leaving Marla no time to notice anything, get more than an impression of nubby orange and dark leather, the smell of old pipe tobacco sunk deep into the fabric and wood. She caught a quick glimpse of a bath through an open door, then was in the bedroom, Bethel tugging at the frame of a massive valet stand against the rear wall, muttering, "Oh, open, you silly thing!"

The mirror over the seat abruptly swung free, into the room; beyond was a solid panel that gave when Bethel pushed on it, opening into a rear corridor. Garman's wife climbed onto the seat, puffing as she worked her considerable bulk through the narrow space, twisting and feeling behind her with her foot until it found the floor. Through, she arranged the strap of her dress.

"Well, Miss Logan? Are you just going to stand there?"

Marla followed her, almost snagging the hem of her robe on the corner of the mirror. Like the corridor above, this one cut across the back of the house, to the service stairs. Through the windows she could see the sky, filled with columns of smoke that slanted against the line of mountains. Then she glanced into the corridor that led to the gallery, and turned that way while Bethel scurried on for the service stairs at the north end of the building.

Marla's discarded slacks and blouse were on the bed, folded neatly; the swimsuit was arranged over the back of a chair, dry now and wrinkled. The slacks made sense if they were to move quickly. She dressed, found her own purse and wallet, grabbed the few pieces of jewelry she owned, and stuffed them into the alligator bag. She hated to leave her clothes, but they could be easily replaced; her life was another matter.

She was almost through the door again when she became aware of the voices: they were in the storeroom, on the other side of the secret panel—arguing, growing louder as they came closer. The volume increased as the panel opened, and then Steiner came through the closet door, his arms burdened with a small but heavy bar of yellow metal.

He stopped. "Miss Doren! What are you doing here?"

"I came to get dressed," said Marla, inanely. She could see the swastika stamp on the bar, in a circle on the breast of an eagle with wings spread. "My clothes—"

"Get out of the way, Steiner!"

Another man pushed through, Steiner stepping aside; he was a stranger, staggering with another bar. Marla knew he was George Gibson even before Garman came from the closet behind his brother.

George Gibson cursed. "What the hell is this? Garman! God damn it, now what do we do?"

Marla took a half-step backward, her fingers brushing the frame of the door as Garman stared, shocked. Like the other two, he carried a bar of gold, arms stiff and shoulders hunched, the weight pulling him forward. As did Helmer, when he popped through. The four of them were nearly jostling one another, crowding the space between the closet and the bed.

"Miss Doren." His eyes narrowed.

"I came for my clothes," Marla said again,

lamely. "I didn't have anything to wear in Corliss's room. . . ."

"God damn it, Garman! The fat's in the fire!"

"Shut up, George!" he said roughly. "I can handle this matter."

"Like you've handled everything else?" jeered his brother. "The way you put every cent the company could scrape together into Europe just in time to be expropriated?"

"Shut up, you fool!" He wheeled on his brother. "I should have let Metz keep you in that damn prison camp!"

"Don't leave, Miss Doren," Steiner said lazily. Unlike the brothers, there was no sign of panic in his voice. "I think we can handle this little problem, Garman." His eyes were hooded; Marla shivered.

"What are you planning?" demanded Garman.

"Just a little accident. A fall down the stairs. A tragic way for such a beautiful young woman to die, but in the situation no one will doubt that she was running."

Marla wanted to scream, but her throat was frozen. She could only stare at the men, her eyes wide in horror as they touched first Garman and then the others. The brothers were grim-faced, the other two professionally objective as they talked about killing her.

"You take care of it, Steiner," said Garman. "George, get the trap open so we can start sending this stiff down into the cellar. I fixed the coal chute so it will go into the well. If the house goes, the gold will be safe under the water until we come back for it."

George moved to the French window, lowering

his bar to the floor, then went onto the little porch and bent over. Marla couldn't see what he did, but a small, square trap door came up; he knelt, peering into the hole, then looked back at his brother.

"You better make sure Bethel and the servants are out of the house, Garman—they might hear the gold going down the chute."

Garman nodded. "All right. We'll have to put her someplace—the Looking Glass; it's as secure as any other place in the house, and appropriate. George and I will take her, Steiner. You two keep bringing the gold into the closet, but keep the door closed—somebody might come looking for her."

"What will you tell them?"

"Nothing. For all we know, she fell through a secret panel."

George laughed, a sharp bark, as Garman turned to deposit his bar inside the closet—and Marla twisted around and broke into the corridor. She heard George shout, heard them pounding after her, panic clutching her heart as she ran for the stairs. From the corner of her eye she saw the bright hotel wagon standing in the drive below, somebody—Jack—shoving something into it. When she passed the next window, Corliss was there.

"You bitch!" George was panting, but he managed the curse through clenched teeth; he was just behind her, and the stairs were just ahead—

Marla's hands slammed into the wall, shocking new pain into her body as her headlong rush came to an abrupt stop. Her vision was swimming; she swayed drunkenly for a crucial few seconds, and he was on her, grabbing her by the hair, yanking her back and twisting cruelly. Marla staggered as he threw her against the wall, and sat down, stunned, hands flat against the floor. She saw his foot coming up toward her face—

Garman: "Don't be stupid, George! We don't want any marks that couldn't have come from the fall."

Thank you, Garman, for stopping him! Then they were dragging her to her feet, Marla unable to stand by herself, and pulling her roughly along a corridor into darkness. She was barely on the edge of consciousness when Garman opened a scraping door, and had passed out when they threw her into the room. She didn't hear the door close again, or feel the pain when her nose smashed against the floor. . . .

The world was hazed with pale pink. Marla blinked, inhaled dust, sneezed, and rolled onto her side, pain stabbing from a score of injuries, old and new. She gasped, pushing with her hands, and managed to come up onto all fours. Some of her hair hung over the top of her head, some down the side of her face, the individual strands blurrily thick against her crossed vision.

She swallowed, spat a hair from her mouth, pushed more away from her eyes. The pink was a cabbage rose in a field of blue; the carpet made her raise her head and look around. The four-poster bed was just out of reach. They had brought her back to Blue South.

Seconds passed while Marla gathered strength; then she pulled herself up onto the padded chest at the foot of the bed, and sat heavily, hands limp over her thighs, staring at the vanity ruffles. Her chest heaved as she brought air into her lungs and expelled old. They were going to kill her, let Steiner kill her. Both of them were letting him do it—either of them could have killed a brother. . . .

Marla raised her head and sat back against the foot of the bed. Her image stared back from the vanity mirror, fright-wigged and filthy, mouth open and eyes wide. If it didn't hurt so much, she'd laugh. . . .

The room was stifling; the men had closed the French windows as well as the door. She twisted around, holding on to the bedpost, and saw the towering columns of smoke from the advancing fire, reaching toward the house. . . .

Something was wrong. The fire was to the north . . . this room looked south. Were there two fires, the house trapped beneath them? But the wind couldn't be coming from two directions at the same time. . . .

Marla turned back, head darting about. The closets were on her right—that was wrong! There were cosmetics on the vanity, but none of her own; everything was reversed, the opposite of the way it should be. She stared at a jar of facial pack, trying to puzzle out the strange printing on the label. The words were big enough, but they didn't make sense.

Marla came off the bench and grabbed the bottle: the words were backward. The other labels were backward too. She held the jar to the mirror and read it easily.

This wasn't her room—it was a mirror image!

Everything was reversed, even the patterns of the carpet and the wallpaper. Garman said it was the Looking Glass . . . another of Beechhaven's practical jokes! Put a guest befuddled with alcohol into bed in Blue South, transfer him while he was asleep to Blue North, and be someplace to watch when he woke up and tried to make sense of the world. (It must have been Gabriel's contribution; Alicia didn't permit alcohol and wouldn't have allowed her husband to do it.) The victims were probably drugged, given a Mickey Finn. Nice people, the Gibsons! Amoral, without social conscience—a pratfall in the movies must strike them as funny, but how much funnier for it to happen in real life, the poor fool slipping on the banana peel really breaking his leg!

(Not all Gibsons are monsters; not Corliss and Skelly. . . .)

Marla tried the door and was not surprised to find it locked; the knob wouldn't even turn or rattle. She turned back to the French windows; at least she could open them, get some ventilation—scream for help!

But they were as solid in their frames as was the door. Desperate, Marla grabbed the facial pack from the vanity and pounded it against one of the panes: nothing. The glass wouldn't even star. The windows were shatterproof, and now she saw that they were thick enough to slightly distort the view beyond.

The closets . . . maybe there was a secret panel from here, too. Guests weren't supposed to know about the one from the twin. But the closet doors were solid panels, and, after wasting too much of her energy, Marla realized that they had no hinges. She went back to the door to the real world and pounded with both fists, shouting, but no one came. . . .

Marla stopped fighting, and slumped across the bed, staring up at the ceiling. It was hopeless: no one could hear her, no one would help her. Incredible! She came here to escape the collapse of her world, to find herself in a nightmare!

Nightmare . . . Please, God, let me be sleeping! She raised her left hand and dug the nails of the other into the flesh of her arm: nothing. She felt the pain, but it was not enough to override the other aches and throbbings. Her extended hands went to her face, drew down her cheeks. . . .

"Ouch!" The bruise beneath her eye was hot, but the pain didn't bring her from the nightmare. She was awake. . . .

The smell of the fire was fainter in this sealed room, but still it managed to penetrate, seeping through invisible cracks and soaking through the fabric of wood and masonry. A fly buzzed suddenly, startling her; it lit on her hand, Marla raising it to stare at the creature. How were you trapped, fellow prisoner?

The fly rubbed its legs together impatiently, then flew off and disappeared above the canopy. She heard it start and stop, but it didn't come back. Marla regretted its antisocial behavior. At least it was alive with her, feeble though it might be as a companion.

Alive . . . What would it be like, dying? She hoped it would be quick. They say a broken neck finishes you, you never know what happened. Andrew, soon you'll have company in your loneliness. . . .

Andrew!

"Andrew! Help me!"

Talking to a ghost. Marla sat up on the edge of the bed, fingertips pressed against her cheeks hollowing her mouth. She watched herself in the mirror, wondering who the mad woman could be.

"Andrew?"

She *must* be out of her mind. Marla managed a small laugh, then closed her mouth, swallowing against dry throat. Talking hurt; she needed water. She needed her head examined. She *must* be out of her mind; how could she have fallen for the children's crazy story? The fly buzzed briefly. What do you think of that, fly? Do flies believe in ghosts? In Heaven and Hell?

The buzzing rasped twice, then cut off, as though he were answering. Marla laughed again, shaking her head. Might as well believe flies could answer, could communicate with humans. It was no more farfetched than believing in ghosts seeking vengeance.

Her breath caught. Her spine was crawling as the chill returned, then moved out. Marla stared at her mirror image, eyes wide with wildness; but even in that instant the madness was softening, leaving them. Her panic was going, a calmness taking its place. No longer distracted by mad ramblings, her body once more paid attention to the thousand pain signals, and to the lack of air in the closed room.

"Andrew?"

Marla knew he was here. She might not believe in him, but something was here. Was that a flicker of movement in the mirror, air currents shifting and almost visible?

232

She was calm as she said, "Andrew, bring the children! I need their help!"

(I know.)

The thought was in her mind, sliding among her own, drifting like vapor across her awareness. It could have been her own, but it was alien: an intruder.

"Hurry, Andrew!"

(I can't reach them.)

Fourteen

Marla slumped in dejection, on the brink of total despair. Her hopes had brought her manically high, to the edge of hysteria; now the drop into the pit was dizzyingly fast, and carried her correspondingly deeper.

(The wall)

The drifting tendril of alien presence moved through the tangle of her thoughts, separating them like threads in a skein, each a sudden mental shout for attention as it was pulled to the forefront, then a whimper as it was shrugged away again, ignored.

(Look there)

The cold was in Marla's chest now; it surrounded her heart, squeezing tight as body hormones depleted blood sugar, a physical reaction, not supernatural. Marla stared blankly at the space of wall between the vanity and the chaise longue, a stretch as wide as the immovable door. Her eyelids dropped once every five seconds in an infinitesimal blackout. . . .

Marla blinked rapidly. Why was that space naked? It seemed empty, when the rest of the room was crowded; there was no equivalent stretch along any of the other walls. The longue was out of position; it should be angled more, moved at least a foot this way. . . .

She rose from the bed, no longer thinking consciously, coming up without effort; her body pains were forgotten, suddenly below the threshold of awareness. Marla moved lightly toward the wall . . . felt as though she were floating. Her feet slid over the top of the carpet pile without crushing the fibers, while her hand rose before her and reached out until a tiny electric shock jumped from the surface of the wall just before contact. Marla could feel the slight unevenness beneath the paper where the paste had lumped, where tiny depressions in the plaster surface had not been properly sanded by the finisher.

Breath sighed out as her other hand came up to measure the wall. Yellow and white roses tumbled across one another, green vines trailing among them in lines so thin that they were almost invisible against the more powerful blue background. Marla watched with interest as her forefinger touched a yellow bud, thumb stretched down to another, little finger angled until it could reach a third.

Her wrist was cocked at an awkward angle as she brought pressure against the wall, then brought up her left hand, pushing against the concealed latch. The panel cracked, Marla releasing the pressure before it completely cleared the wall; there it stopped, hung up.

She pushed again with her left hand, and heard again the scraping noise the panel had made when Garman and George had brought her here. The panel opened easily the rest of the way and she pushed through.

Thank you, Andrew!

Even if he didn't exist, Marla had decided to believe in him. Who else could have directed her to the one way out of the prison?

She was in an attic—the main attic. The ceiling rose to a peak above her, rafters and massive support beams sloping inward almost to the floor. There were hips in the roof, and flat places; near the peak, a skylight spilled a brief flash of sunlight before the wind rolled the fire column across the sky, closing the break.

For the first time, Marla was aware of the wind. It howled around the roof, whistling, rattling. Something over her head broke loose and began a scraping slide to freedom. One of the slates, she decided. How close was the fire? With this wind, it would tear through the house with almost nothing to stop it.

The attic was as big as the house below from front to rear, and reached across a third of the width; there it was cut by an unfinished wall, but Marla could see a door leading into the next compartment.

The space was too large to have filled even with sixty years of clutter and junk; there were scattered and random heaps and piles. Marla saw a broken child's rocking horse and a sagging and rusting playground set; there, a stack of old mattresses; nearby, scuffed trunks and a pair of sawhorses supporting a weathered two-by-twelve plank. Unidentifiable heaps—some of the piles were fifteen or twenty feet apart.

How to get out of here? There were gables along the lower reaches, alleviating the gloom; in the distance she could see the forest line and the

road where it topped the second knoll. Toward
the front of the house she saw the curved wall of
the tower cutting through the roofline as it followed its own architectural impulses. A well
there, must be a staircase; but did she want to go
that way?

There: another slash against the back—that
must be the way they'd brought her. She moved
that way, and was almost there when she heard
voices below. One was arguing, angry: unmistak-
ably George Gibson. Then Steiner's guttural sar-
casm cut him off.

They were coming for her!

Marla wheeled around, frantic: the door to the
rest of the attic? She took one tentative step, but
there wasn't time. The tower . . . there was no
other way!

She ran, heart pounding and lungs fighting for
breath, tennis shoes almost silent as they crossed
the board floor. Thank God for that much! A
board rail protected the well; she dropped into
the stairs, and ducked out of sight as George
Gibson's head rose into view at the rear of the attic. Her eyes swept across the panel of the hidden
room—dear God, she had left it open! They'd
know instantly that she was out!

The stairs followed the curve of the wall, and
Marla dropped down as she heard George's shout.
Then his footsteps pounded, and she hurried
down a dozen feet until she ran into a blind wall.

Oh! Marla wiped her mouth and brushed hair
from her eyes. A simple door was cut into the
wall of the tower, an old-fashioned lift latch for a
handle. She could hear George arguing with

237

Steiner—they'd be coming here in another minute. Go back and be caught—

She went forward, lifting the latch and pushing the door, wincing as a hinge squeaked. She turned quickly and shut it again, still a door on this side and not one of the foolish secret panels. Then she looked for a bolt or a lock, but there was none.

Marla turned back, leaning against the door; she was in Alicia Gibson's bedroom—Alicia was staring at her in shock, from where she was packing clothes into a steamer trunk. Boy's clothing.

Alicia found her voice. "What is the meaning of this, Miss Doren?"

"I'm sorry, Mrs. Gibson. They're after me."

"After you?" Alicia stared as though Marla were something that had just revealed itself to be repulsive. "Who? And why?"

Before Marla could answer, she heard feet pounding down the stairs and felt the jar as a heavy body hit the door, slamming the latch and pushing it open. One of the men cursed, hit the door again, then brought pressure.

Marla was too light to stand against them, although she tried, looking over her shoulder at Alicia.

"Please, Mrs. Gibson! You must help me—"

She went staggering, and almost fell over a chair as the door flew open and Steiner and Helmer came in. They gave Alicia one quick look, then headed for Marla.

"What is this?" demanded Alicia, almost screaming. "Who are you men? What are you doing? *George!*"

Shock upon shock was too much. Alicia clutched her heart, moaning, and staggered to a chair. George wiped his mouth, glaring angrily at Marla, who was now in the hands of the other two; then he went to his mother.

"Mother!" He raised her chin. "Are you all right?"

"Oh! Oh merciful God in Heaven! Tell me this is all a nightmare!"

"It's real, Mother. A nightmare, but real."

Garman came out of the attic door, scowling at his brother and at the other two. Through the glass wall, Marla saw a tongue of flame suddenly advance to the far side of the lake. Steiner and Garman saw it too.

Marla winced as Steiner brought pressure on her already bruised arm, mistaking her surrender as another attempt to break free. She looked around, seeing the bedroom for the first time since stumbling through the door. Unlike the level below, Alicia had decorated her bedroom in an earlier style, undistinguished; the heavy pieces were almost Victorian, might have come from Grand Rapids at the turn of the century. They suited her better than the ultramodern furnishings below.

Alicia moaned as George supported her, shaking her head again and again.

"I don't understand! What is happening, Garman? Who are those men—how did George—oh, dear God!"

"Mrs. Gibson!" It was Steiner, voice cracking with authority. "You must listen. This is most regrettable; it should not have happened, but it has,

239

and nothing can be done. I suggest you leave now. Garman will take you to the railroad."

Alicia straightened. "Garman, who is that man?"

"A business associate," Steiner said smoothly. "Time is very short, Mrs. Gibson. You must leave now."

"Why are you holding Miss Doren?" she asked sharply.

"The matter does not concern you. I am told you have a cool head, Mrs. Gibson. Use it."

"I'm not going," said Alicia. "I don't know what this is all about, but I intend to find out. Take your hands off the girl!"

Steiner shrugged and glanced at Garman. "Talk sense to her, Garman."

George spoke first. "Mother, you must keep quiet! They'll kill you too!"

"*Kill* me?" Alicia laughed. "Oh, now I know this is only a dream!"

George shook his head and bit his lip. "They mean it. They'll do *anything*—they're Nazis, Mother! For almost a year they've forced Garman and me to smuggle their stolen gold and art treasures into this country—most of it from people we knew! People you've entertained right here! But they're dead now, all of them, and we'll be dead with them if you don't do what they say!"

George was on the verge of hysteria; Marla saw the disgust in Steiner and Helmer—Germans, Austrians, the nationality made no difference. Nazis . . . she was the one to feel disgusted.

"There will be no killing," Alicia said firmly. "I won't permit it."

George laughed. "How are you going to stop them—the way you stopped Garman twenty-five years ago?"

Alicia flinched, her face paling. "You don't know what you're saying, George. . . ."

"Oh, I know, Mother. I was there, remember? I saw Garman do it, saw him kick Gabe's foot out from beneath him, saw him roll Gabe into the water. And you saw it, too—I knew you were watching us from the house. I'm eagle-eye George, remember? Let them kill the girl—what's one more murder on your conscience? If you have a conscience."

Every hair on Marla's neck was standing tense: the room was suddenly ice-cold. The others felt it too; Helmer was shivering and jerking his shoulder. Only the Gibsons ignored the phenomenon.

Then the sensation was gone, and Marla knew that Andrew had left. Was he satisfied? No . . . Garman remained unpunished. Would not be punished . . .

Steiner said, "Garman, we're wasting time. If we delay here any longer we'll all be caught by the fire. Settle this matter or I will settle it for you. Two can accidentally die as easily as one; more easily—they can be found together."

"What about George?" said Helmer. "I warned you he was a coward. Eliminate the three of them—no one but Garman knows he's here, so no one will even look for his body."

"Garman?" Steiner raised an eyebrow. "Do you object? I agree with *Standartenführer* Helmer: George has outlived his usefulness."

Still Garman hesitated, looking from his

mother to his brother. Marla could almost hear the wheels turning in his mechanical mind, and saw the answer in his eyes before he turned to his mother and spoke.

"I'm sorry, Mother." Alicia stiffened. "My life is in this—I won't see everything lost. The company is ruined, there's no way to survive the war, but with the Jew gold we can come out almost even."

His mother slumped in her chair, shaking her head. "I knew twenty-five years ago I was wrong, but how could I turn in my own flesh, my own blood? Gabriel was my son, my first son, but I suffered his murder in silence, *in silence!* Why? Why?"

"Garman—"

"Shut up, George!" Ice was in his eyes. "God, but I'm sick of your whining. Thirty years of it is enough. I'm glad it's over."

He wheeled and started toward the attic door. Marla saw George fumble in his jacket, and felt Helmer move before she saw him, from the corner of her eye, drawing a gun, and in the same instant she heard the crash of a door below and Tim shouting:

"Marla! Where are you?"

Time was frozen for eternity while Marla sucked in breath for her scream, Garman wheeling again, staring at the Nazis. Then her shout exploded across the room:

"Tim! Watch out—don't come up—"

Steiner rabbit-punched her, but he was distracted as George drew his gun: two weapons barked at once, George's and Helmer's. The blow glanced across the back of Marla's skull, bringing scream-

242

ing pain from the old bruise. Stunned, she sagged; but blood appeared against Steiner's shoulder, blossoming into a black-red stain.

Steiner cursed, released her, and staggered back. Marla fell, cracking one knee, but caught herself on all fours. Garman wheeled again, running for the stairs—then stopped as suddenly, backing away, hands slowly rising. Marla raised her aching head to see Davis coming through the attic door, monstrous double-barreled shotgun in his hand.

"Now you just better take it easy, Mr. Garman. You don't want to go no place till we find out what's goin' on around here."

"Motherrrrrrrrrrrrrrr!"

The scream tore from George's throat as he stared at the bloody hole in his stomach. He clutched the wound, his gun dipping to point toward the floor, his knees sagging; he fell forward, kneeling and crying as his life drained from his belly. Again the cry came, a whisper barely heard: *"Mother!"* Then George fell over.

Things were happening too quickly. Marla saw Helmer bring his pistol against Davis; she lunged for his leg—and screamed when his kick missed her head and caught her shoulder. But he was off-balance, staggering back, and now Tim rose through the floor, coming up the circular staircase, an improbably huge automatic in his hand.

"Drop it!" he said, trying to take in everything. "Army Intelligence!"

Helmer fired again, still off-balance, and Tim's .45 bucked once. The Nazi's bullet whistled past Garman, passed within inches of Davis's ear. The sound shocked him; the shotgun wavered, and

Garman grabbed the barrel, pulling Davis around to block Tim's shot as he wrested the gun from his hands. Before Tim could come all the way into the room, Garman had the shotgun reversed, aimed toward Marla.

"Hold it, Layard! Drop the gun, or the girl gets the first barrel."

"No!" Marla raised one hand. "Tim, don't listen to him!"

But Tim was backing off, not dropping his gun but lowering it to his side. From the corner of her eye Marla saw Helmer sag against the bed, his face drained of blood. His stare was blank. Then he toppled to the floor.

"It's over, Garman," said Tim. "You're finished. We've been on to you for over a year. Give it up now, while you still have a chance."

Garman laughed. "What chance? What's the charge—treason? In wartime they shoot traitors, don't they? Stay there!"

"Be sensible, man—you can't get away!"

"Maybe not, but I'm going to try."

He was through the door, pulling it shut; they heard him pound up the stairs, Tim coming the rest of the way into the room. Davis rubbed his wrist, then looked at the younger man; he started to apologize, but Tim cut him off.

"Take Helmer's gun, Davis. Watch Steiner!"

Tim had reached the door when they heard the shotgun blast. He winced; but there was only the one shot. Then Garman was running, his feet pounding away.

Tim opened the door. "Jack! You okay?" he called.

Marla heard the call from the other side of the

244

attic: "He didn't get me, Tim. He's going out on the roof."

Tim pounded up the stairs, leaving Davis to guard Steiner. Marla heard him shout, "Garman! You damn fool, come back!"

Alicia was staring at her; Marla felt embarrassed as the old woman, looking every minute of her age, slowly shook her head.

"How can you turn your own flesh, your own blood, over to the police?" She was speaking only to herself. "They would have sent him away, locked him in with crazy people! I couldn't do that. . . ."

Alicia was rocking now, moaning, in her straight chair, legs tucked beneath her, upper body moving back and forth. Marla approached her warily, afraid of the mad look in her eyes. She touched Alicia's shoulder.

"Mrs. Gibson! Remember the children."

Alicia cocked her head a trifle, looking at her. "The children? I have no children. Gabriel is dead. George is dead. Garman is dead. I have no children."

"Corliss and Skelly!" said Marla. "They need you!"

A shudder passed across the frail frame. Alicia passed a hand across her eyes, shook her head; the look of insanity was gone. She spoke again, in an almost normal tone.

"Yes, Miss Doren, you're right. The children are what matter. What's done is done."

Lightning cracked suddenly, the actinic glare painting the room stark, bleaching the color until it could have been the room below. Thunder followed immediately, the roar shaking the fabric of the house, and almost immediately rain began to pelt against the glass wall. Stunned yet fascinated, Marla approached the window, no longer able to see the columns of smoke across the lake. She pressed her face against the glass, felt an icy chill as lightning again split the heavens, and turned to see Garman perilously near the edge of the roof.

He was drenched, fighting to keep his balance on the suddenly slippery slates, staggering back to relative safety. He was above Marla but no more than fifty feet away; she saw clearly the white face of the boy behind him, the gash of his mouth when he spoke. Garman turned, saw the youngster in old-fashioned clothes, and took a step back, shaking his head. Another step, and his foot went out from beneath him: Marla saw the slate fly into the storm. Garman scrabbled wildly, the gun falling from his hands to bounce over the edge of the roof, and then he went after it, cartwheeling twice before he struck the roof of the porch.

Marla turned away, shuddering . . . but not before the boy vanished as suddenly as he had appeared.

Andrew's spirit was free. His murderer was punished.

Afterword

Marla came out of the house as Davis swung Tim's bag into the buggy, refusing to let him handle it himself. His uniform was pressed, the lieutenant's bars shining on his shoulders.

"Well." He looked at her, sober. "This is it, Marla. No more stalling. I have to get back to Washington."

"Where will you go next?"

"I don't know. I've requested combat training, but Intelligence never likes to let a warm body go. There's talk of sending me to language school in Texas. Do you think you'd like Texas?"

"Will we have time for a honeymoon?"

"At least seventy-two hours."

"That seems reasonable." She nodded. "Anything I can't stand, it's a man who doesn't know when to get out of the house."

Tim laughed, grabbing her. "You mean it? You will marry me?"

"Was there ever any doubt in your mind?"

"Not for a minute!"

His lips crushed hers then, Tim holding her tight until Marla could no longer breathe. But she didn't care, she wanted this moment to last. He was the one who finally broke the embrace.

"It'll take a month or two, maybe more, before I work through the paperwork from this mess, Marla. Are you sure you want to stay?"

"The children need someone, Tim. Bethel is ready to go back to New York, but they won't really miss her." She moved to the edge of the porte cochere and looked up at the tower wall; Alicia was there, looking down at them. "Alicia needs someone. I'll stay, for a while."

"Only until we can be together permanently."

Marla smiled, sensing the presences behind her. She turned and saw Corliss and Skelly standing just within the door. They were dressed in their best, scrubbed for tea with their grandmother. She glanced at her watch: four o'clock.

"What are you two doing here? You know your grandmother doesn't like to be kept waiting."

"We wanted to say good-bye to Tim," said Skelly.

They came rushing out and threw their arms around him. "Oh, Tim!" cried Corliss. "You will come back to see us, won't you?"

He laughed. "I have to come back, outlaws. How else can I see my wife?"

He looked at Marla again, reached for her hand, and pressed it tight. "I'll write as soon as I get things straightened out, Marla."

"I'll write every day...."

He vaulted into the buggy and Davis flicked the reins. Marla stood with the children, her arms around their shoulders, watching until the horse-drawn buggy took Tim around the corner....

But not out of her life.

Never again would he go out of her life.

"Well!" She hugged the children. Five days

248

since the end of the world for their father . . . but not for them. Alicia was the Gibson fortune; no more than half her money had been in the operation Garman had destroyed. This house, all the family homes, still belonged to her . . . and would in time belong to Skelly and Corliss.

"Inside, you two! Don't dawdle. And don't spoil your supper with her cookies!" she called, as they ran along the porch. She watched them until they went in the other door, then turned to look over the lake. Andrew's lake. Her lake, now. Alicia had already promised a wedding present: a choice site for a summer home, almost within shouting distance of the big house. Tim would like that; she knew he would. . . .